Praise for Andrew Grey

MW00696267

The Best Revenge

…an intricate story about two inspiring men who instead of giving up teach us that living well, is in the end, the best revenge of all. Come read this phenomenal story that kept me spell bound from the start.
~5 Angels and a Recommended Read from Fallen Angel Reviews

…a completely delightful story of two people who find love even as problems from the past, present and an uncertain future loom. This author weaves a spell around you and completely captivates you from start to finish. With intriguing characters, a fast moving plot and some tender and loving sex scenes, Mr. Grey delivers a powerful story that leaves you breathless.
~5 Hearts from Love Romances and More

Bottled Up

I came to care about these characters and I cheered them on to the end.
~4 ½ Blue Ribbons from Romance Junkies

Thursday's Child

…the experience of discovery of this beautiful world is so refreshing… a perfect read after a stressful, chaotic day. I highly recommend it!
~4 ½ Stars from Rainbow Reviews

There are definitely twists I didn't see coming that kept my attention and made the story anything but predictable. His ability to mingle folklore with reality while adding romance and suspense has made **Mr. Grey's** books climb to the top of my must read list.
~5 Angels from Fallen Angel Reviews

Love Means...
No Shame

ANDREW GREY

Dreamspinner Press

Published by
Dreamspinner Press
4760 Preston Road
Suite 244-149
Frisco, TX 75034
http://www.dreamspinnerpress.com/

Love Means... No Shame

Cover Design by Mara McKennen

ISBN: 978-1-61581-057-4

Printed in the United States of America
First Edition
September, 2009

eBook edition available
eBook ISBN: 978-1-61581-058-1

To everyone in CPRW, I'm so glad I found you.

To Dominic, the love of my life,
without whose support I couldn't do any of this.

And to the staff at Dreamspinner Press,
for everything you do to make me look good.
You're the best.

CHAPTER 1

GEOFF LAUGHTON woke in a strange bed, light streaming through the windows, a huge, hot, sweaty body next to him. His head pounded and his ass hurt. "That was one hell of a night," he muttered to himself as he forced his legs to move. Sitting on the edge of the bed, head cradled in his hands, he tried to think where he was. Oh yeah, he'd gone out dancing last night with Lonnie and Juan.

He turned to the man lying prone on the bed. "God...." He remembered—well, at least parts of it. Tequila shooters followed by dancing with a tree. "That must be him." Like it usually did, the rest came back to him in a rush: dancing, him climbing his dance partner. Hell, he'd even stuck his hand down the guy's pants.

His head throbbed again, and he made himself get to his feet to stumble to the bathroom. He didn't bother to turn on the light, probably couldn't find it anyway, and managed to make it to the sink. Turning on the tap, he put his hands under the cool water and splashed his face, groaning with relief as the water tingled on his skin. "At least I'm alive." Turning off the water, he used the facilities and then walked a little more steadily back into the bedroom to find his bed partner awake and groaning.

"What day is it?" He was holding his head and moaning softly. "Fuck, I hate tequila." He looked up at Geoff, eyes as red as Geoff's had been when he'd seen them in the mirror.

"Sunday, thank God." Geoff started looking around for his clothes, finding his pants near the bed and pulling them on.

"Easy for you to say. I gotta go to work." The huge man looked at the clock. "Fuck… gotta be there in half an hour." He lifted himself to his feet and shuffled toward the bathroom, the door closing softly, very softly.

Geoff searched the room and managed to find the rest of his clothes. After dressing, he definitely didn't want to move too quickly. He shuffled in the general direction of the kitchen.

"There is a god." The coffee maker was plugged in and set. Geoff pressed the start button, and the machine took over and was soon filling the space with the heavenly smell of fresh brewed.

Geoff heard the shower start and then stop a few minutes later. Searching the cupboards, he found two cups. They appeared clean, unlike the rest of the apartment, and he waited until the coffee was finished before filling the cups and walking back to the bedroom.

The door was part way open and… ummm, Gary… yeah, that was his name, Gary… was getting dressed. Pushing open the door, Geoff quietly handed Gary a filled mug.

"Thanks, dude, I really need this." Gary sipped the drink and put the mug on the table. "I gotta be gone in about two minutes."

Geoff nodded, sipped his coffee—damn, that was good—and turned around, letting Gary finish getting ready. By the time Gary emerged from the bedroom, Geoff had finished his coffee and felt vaguely human again. "Thanks, Gary, I'll see you around."

"Yeah, dude… thanks."

Gary was still finishing his coffee as Geoff left the apartment and headed down the stairs to the front door of the seventies-era apartment building. Once outside, the air helped to clear his head, and he searched the parking lot for his car, finding it right across the way.

Fishing his keys out of his pocket and getting in, he started the car, pulling out of the space and heading toward home—well, what passed for home, anyway.

His old car managed to get him there, and he parked in his reserved spot and headed up the walk to his building. It was newer than the one he'd just left: eighties chic instead of seventies. He let himself in and went up the stairs to his apartment.

Inside, there wasn't much: a sofa, a chair, and a television on a stand. Geoff tossed his keys on the counter and looked longingly to the bathroom. He had to wash the smell of booze, sweat, and spunk off his body. Geoff headed straight to his bedroom, which was furnished in the same sparse manner as the rest of the apartment: just a bed and a dresser. Stripping off his clothes, he went into the bathroom. He made the mistake of turning on the light and looking in the mirror. "Fuck." His eyes were dark and his skin pasty. "The mirror never lies, does it?"

Geoff began cleaning up, brushing his teeth and shaving before starting the water and stepping beneath the spray. The shower felt good—cleansing, refreshing. He started to scrub, and he could almost feel the remnants of the last night washing down the drain.

The phone was ringing as he got out of the shower. Wrapping a towel around his waist, he raced to answer it.

"Geoff, it's Raine. How's the hangover?"

Geoff knew that Raine had purposely started talking loudly. "Bastard." He heard laughter on the other end of the phone.

"Actually, it's not so bad… not as bad as it *could* be, anyway. How's yours?"

There was more laughter on the end of the line. "I don't get hangovers, remember?" It was one of life's cruel fates. Raine could drink like a fish and never seemed to feel anything the next morning. "You want to meet for coffee?"

"Sure, give me fifteen. I'll meet you around the corner." Geoff dried himself and dressed, putting on a sweatshirt against the spring chill in the air, and left the apartment, walking happily to the corner.

The coffee shop was packed, but he spied Raine's head of jet black, curly hair at one of the tables, and he headed that way.

"I didn't get anything. If I get up, I'll lose the table," Raine said.

"No problem, I'll get what you want. Large latte?"

Raine nodded and smiled his agreement, so Geoff got in line. It took a while, but he finally returned to the table with coffees and two large sticky buns. Sugar. He needed sugar.

"Thanks, Geoff." Raine took the offered cup, and Geoff sat down. "You look like hell." Raine sipped his coffee.

"Gee, thanks. Don't sugarcoat it."

Raine laughed. "Well, you do." The man was always blunt and to the point. If nothing else, you always knew where you stood with him, because he held nothing back. "You've been burning the candle at both ends for a while."

"I know." Geoff had been. Since he arrived six months earlier, fresh out of college with a degree in accounting and a libido on overdrive, he'd almost made a mission out of seeing how many men he could have, and it was wearing thin.

Raine continued sipping his coffee. "You need to take it easy, relax a little. You can't screw your way to happiness." There it was—one of Raine's witticisms. The man had one for all occasions.

"No, but you can have a lot of fun trying," the two said in unison. They laughed merrily, breaking Geoff out of his mood. Raine was good for his soul. No matter how bad things got, he could always count on Raine's easy manner and carefree humor to break him out of a funk.

"Seriously, Geoff, you're going overboard with the man buffet."

"I know."

They finished their coffee and sticky buns. "Let's catch a movie and have some fun. I think you could use it," Raine commented.

Geoff checked his imaginary calendar. "Well, I've got such a busy day planned, cleaning the apartment, laundry; I don't know how I'll fit it in."

"Sarcasm is unbecoming." They both laughed and cleaned up their table before leaving the coffee shop.

Geoff and Raine spent the rest of the day together, going to a movie and doing a little shopping. Since they were both fairly broke, they looked more than shopped and then went back to Raine's apartment and spent the evening watching movies until Geoff headed home, where he fell into bed.

GEOFF had to be at his office by eight on Monday morning, and he was nearly late. Unlike most of the past few weeks, he'd slept well and hadn't spent Sunday night trolling for men. Arriving just in time, he quietly put his things away and booted up his PC, getting right to work. He'd gotten this job right out of college, working as a staff accountant for a chain of retail stores. He liked the work, and the people he worked with were nice, but most of them were older, and it was difficult to make friends. The one exception had been Raine. He'd met him the first day on the job, and they'd become fast friends. Unfortunately, he was the only real friend Geoff had made. Oh, there were acquaintances and people he went out with, but Raine was his only true friend, which made for a lonely life.

He was busy working on the accounts payable ledger, trying to find an imbalance, when heard a soft cough. "Geoff, Kenny would like to see you in his office."

Kenny was the head of accounting, and when he summoned, you hopped to it. He was a nice guy but demanded punctuality from all his people, and being late when he called was viewed as a sign of disrespect.

An hour later Geoff returned with more mysteries to solve. This was what he loved, really loved. Numbers sang to him, and he had a talent for digging in and finding mistakes and imbalances no matter how small. In a very short time, he'd developed a reputation as someone who could locate small errors before they became big ones.

The one thing he didn't like about his job was that it tended to be very solitary. He spent most of his days working with numbers and very little of his days working with people. He'd really like to do both.

At noon, Raine came to his cubicle, and the two of them had a quick lunch before heading to the company fitness center to work off some of the weekend's excesses. Once they'd changed, they each got on a treadmill and started walking. The room was empty except for them, which was normal.

"I'm thinking of looking for a new job," Raine mentioned.

"Why?" The thought sent chill through Geoff—what would he do without seeing Raine every day?

"I'm not going to go anywhere here. Kenny doesn't really like me, so nothing is gonna happen for me." Raine had been there a year longer than Geoff, but Geoff seemed to get better assignments and more recognition. Geoff didn't know what to say, so he kept walking, increasing the pace of his machine. Raine must have seen the worried look on Geoff's face. "Don't worry, we'll always be friends."

"I know… it's just that this place will be so dull without you."

"Not that Kenny will see it that way, but it probably will be." Modesty wasn't one of Raine's personality attributes. "You going out tonight?"

"No. I decided I'm going to cut back and find other things to do." He'd been drinking way too much lately, and his liver and budget could both use a break. "Maybe tomorrow night." One could stay inside just so much.

Raine started laughing. "You had me worried for a second." They both laughed companionably and finished their workouts.

The small locker room was empty when they got done. Geoff stripped off his sweaty clothes and headed for a quick shower. He'd just started the water when he felt a snap on his butt. "Jesus!" His ass stung where Raine had towel-snapped him. Geoff twisted his towel and snapped it in retaliation, but Raine ducked out of the way. They were both laughing as Geoff climbed in the shower and rinsed off, rubbing his sore cheeks.

Getting out of the shower, he dried off and got dressed. Raine was waiting, and together they walked back to their work area.

Geoff went right back to work, combing the ledger for the error he knew was there… somewhere. He could hear the room buzzing, soft voices talking animatedly, but paid no attention.

7

Rumors flew through the place with the speed of a bullet, but he made a special effort to stay out of the rumor mill.

He'd just found the error and was logging into the system to correct it when he heard a soft knock on his cubicle wall. It was Angela, the director of accounts payable.

"Geoff, I want to introduce you to Garrett Foster, the new AP manager." Geoff stood up and greeted his new boss, extending his hand and looking into the man's eyes. Jesus Christ… he almost pulled his hand back but restrained himself, checking that he was keeping his expression even.

"Good to meet you, Garrett."

The tall blond flashed a brilliant smile, "Looking forward to working with you, Geoff." Taking Geoff's hand, he held it a little longer than he should have and then let go. Geoff had to stop himself from shivering. Then, with one of her bright, fake smiles, Angela led Garrett off to meet the rest of the team.

Geoff collapsed back into his chair, and a few minutes later Raine was standing in front of his desk. "Was that…?"

Geoff nodded slowly. "Mr. Vain himself, yup."

Raine started to chuckle and covered his mouth with his hand to keep from laughing out loud. "Your boss is Mr. Vain."

Geoff held his head in his hand. "Oh God, I knew this was going to catch up with me someday."

Raine leaned close. "Who knew it would be so soon?" Raine gave him his best sympathetic look. "Sorry, man." Then he was gone.

Geoff tried to concentrate but couldn't. His new boss, Garrett Foster, was a guy he'd gone home with about a month earlier. They'd had a reasonably good time, but Garrett—at the time, his name was Phillip—had been a rather selfish lover. His bedroom was covered with mirrors! He and Raine called him Mr. Vain because the song was *so* about him. The man never passed a mirror he didn't like. Geoff wasn't interested in seeing him again, and Garrett being his boss was an added complication Geoff didn't want.

At quitting time, Raine was at his desk right away, and Geoff packed up his things so they could leave as quickly as possible. "Wanna go for dinner?"

Geoff didn't really feel like going anywhere. "I'm just going to go home." *You get what you put out.*

"Then let's get a pizza delivered and veg out." Raine knew what Geoff needed, even if Geoff didn't.

"Okay." They made their way out of the building and back to Geoff's place, where they ordered a pizza. They'd just finished eating when the phone rang.

"Geoff, it's Len." The man sounded choked up, and Geoff stiffened. "It's about your dad."

His father had been fighting cancer for a while, but the last time Geoff had spoken to him, he'd said he was feeling really good. "Do you need me to come home?" Geoff asked.

"Yes." Len's voice broke. "Geoff, he passed away." He heard tears coming from the other end of the line, and he felt his own well up in his eyes as a huge lump swelled in his throat.

"I'll be there as soon as I can." Geoff hung up and turned to Raine, his lower lip quivering as he tried to maintain control of himself. "It's my dad. He passed away this afternoon." Raine pulled him to his chest and hugged him, letting Geoff cry on his shoulder.

Once the tears subsided, Raine spurred into action. "You need to get home. Are you gonna drive or fly?"

Geoff wiped his eyes on his sleeve, "I'd better drive. It'll be just as fast."

"Then we better get you packed. And don't worry about work; I'll talk to Kenny in the morning and tell him what happened. You can call him when you get a chance." By the time Raine left, Geoff was packed, and the car was loaded. All he needed to do was call Len back and start driving first thing in the morning.

CHAPTER 2

THE farm didn't look any different when he crested the rise that gave him the first view of the house, silos, and barn. Well, in the Midwest it was a farm. If it were in the West it would be called a ranch. Stopping the car, he got out and surveyed the view. No, it didn't look any different. The cattle dotted the fields, and he could even see some of the horses in their corrals around the barn.

But it felt different. He knew his dad wouldn't be rushing out to greet him as he always did, pulling him into a bear hug. He also knew that the kitchen wouldn't smell like fresh-baked bread and the bathroom like his father's Old Spice aftershave. "Wow," he breathed to himself as he looked over his family home with a sense of deep sadness.

After taking a deep breath, he got back in the car and drove the remaining distance to the house, pulling between the square brick columns topped with lights and into the long driveway. Stopping the car, he turned off the engine. As soon as he opened the door, he was accosted by three dogs who ran from the porch as fast as their old legs would carry them.

"Hey, boys, how are you?" Geoff knelt down, giving out pats and scratches, getting wet dog kisses and wagged tails in return. It was all he could do not to break down into tears right there.

The screen door closed with a bang. "Your dad loved those mutts almost as much as you." Geoff stood back up as Len walked down the porch steps and hurried to the car. Then Geoff was drawn into a deep, familiar, and loving hug that broke down the last of his resistance, and the dam inside him burst. Huge tears rolled down his cheeks and soaked into Len's shirt as he sobbed against his shoulder.

When the flood subsided, they pulled apart, both wiping their eyes with their hands before walking together up the steps to the huge porch. "What happened, Len? He seemed to be doing so well when I was home the last time."

"Come on inside. I've got lunch on, and we'll talk." Len opened the screen door and ushered Geoff inside.

As usual, they walked right through the sun porch and the huge living room to the kitchen. Geoff sat at the table, the same one he'd sat at when he was a child. "That smells so good, Len."

"I made your favorite pancakes. They're not the same as your dad's, but they're pretty good." A stack was set in front of him, along with strong coffee, butter, real maple syrup, and everything else that made this a home. This was Geoff's favorite meal of all time.

He tried not to think too much and forced himself to eat. As soon as that first bite hit his mouth and the syrup slid down his throat, he relaxed a little—he was home. This tasted like home. The grief threatened to well up again, but he pushed it back. He hadn't realized he was hungry until he started to eat, and then his appetite came back with a vengeance. Len brought his own plate to the table, and they ate in silence, each lost in his own thoughts. "We have an appointment at the funeral home this afternoon at two."

Geoff continued eating. "Okay." Thankfully, that was all Len said while they ate, leaving them both alone with their thoughts. Once he'd finished the plate of pancakes, he felt better, a little stronger and a little more in control of his emotions, although the grief was still right below the surface.

Getting up from the table, he put his dishes in the sink and started running the water to wash them.

"I'll take care of those."

Geoff smiled and mimicked his dad. "House rule number one: if you cook, you don't do dishes." Len and Geoff both smiled slightly as the familiar words washed over them.

Len finished his food and brought the dishes to the sink. "I'm going to check that everything's okay outside, and then we need to talk. I won't be long." Then he was out the back door, and Geoff watched as he strode across the lawn on his way to the barns.

Len and his dad had been together as far back as Geoff could remember. Geoff's mother died when he was about six months and eighteen months later, his dad met Len, and that was that. They'd been together for twenty years. As a child, he'd always called him Len, but he was as much a father as his own had been. It was Len who had taught him to ride his first horse, and it was Len who'd tended his scraped knees. Geoff let out a long breath. "I was really blessed."

Pulling his attention back to the sink, he finished the dishes, setting them in the rack to dry. Len was still in the barns, so Geoff wandered through the familiar rooms of the house. The living room was comfortable, the walls covered with framed pictures. Geoff looked at the photograph of him as a child, riding his first pony with Len and his dad on either side of him, both looking so proud. Next to it was a picture of his dad and Len, so young and handsome, both of them smiling widely, their arms around each other's shoulders.

Len's voice brought Geoff back to the present. "That was shortly after we met."

Geoff took the photograph from the wall. "You can see the love even in the photograph." He'd never noticed it before, but it was there as plain as day.

Len took the photograph and traced the outline of Geoff's dad. "Cliff was special. I knew as soon as I saw him that I loved him." A tear rolled down the tanned cheek. "This picture was taken the day we first made love under a tree at the edge of the creek."

When Geoff was younger, the thought of his parents having sex had just been gross, but as he got older and helped his father breed animals, his attitude had changed. There were nights as a teenager when the windows were open that he could hear his dad and Len in their big bed. They'd always tried to be quiet, but he'd heard them nonetheless.

Len hung the picture back on the wall and sat down in his chair. "There are some things we need to talk about."

Geoff sat down in the chair next to him. "What happened?"

"The cancer kept progressing, and the treatments weren't helping, so he stopped them just after you left the last time." Len's voice was steady, and Geoff wondered how he could do it. "As the weeks went by, the disease progressed. As he got weaker, the pain got stronger; most days he could barely get out of bed. Then, two days ago, I woke to find him up, dressed, and downstairs in the kitchen baking bread." Len stopped talking, and Geoff waited for him to continue. "That was when I knew."

"Knew what?" But he got no response. "Len?"

"Your father and I talked about this when he was first diagnosed." Len seemed so detached.

"What happened?"

"We spent the day together, sitting in these chairs, talking and reminiscing, just the two of us. He seemed like himself again, but I knew that this was his last effort, his Indian summer, if you will. That night we went to bed together, and when we woke up, he could barely raise his head." Len sniffled a little.

"I let him sleep, and later he managed to get out of bed and moved to the sofa in the upstairs sitting room. That was where I found him when I brought him his medication." Len's detached look remained, and Geoff knew something wasn't quite right.

"Len, what is it that my father didn't want me to know?" Len's head whipsawed to Geoff, and then he smiled weakly.

"Your dad didn't want me to tell you." That was his dad, always protecting him.

"What else happened?" Geoff knew Len wouldn't lie to him, but he would leave things out if he thought Geoff would be hurt by them.

Len straightened in his chair. "We talked about this when he was first diagnosed."

"Talked about what?" Geoff knew his dad pretty well, but he had no idea where Len was leading.

"Geoff, the pain at the end was severe. The medication only took the edge off." Tears were running down his cheeks. "Your father cried and begged for the pain to stop. So I helped him back to bed and left his pain medication on the table, and while I was making breakfast, he swallowed the entire bottle."

Geoff sat there stunned. "Why didn't he...?"

"He knew he wouldn't be able to do it if you were here. Can you ever forgive me?" Len broke down and sobbed into his hands.

"There's nothing to forgive." Geoff got up and knelt by Len's chair, hugging the man who'd helped raise him. "What would he have had—a few more weeks of pain and suffering? Why should you treat him with less humanity than we'd treat one of the horses?" Geoff was crying as well, but he knew he had to get this out. "What you did showed love, real love, and I don't know if I'd have had the strength to do what you did for him."

"You don't blame me?"

Geoff shook his head. "No, he died of cancer, pure and simple. If I need to blame anything, I'll blame that." Geoff handed Len a tissue.

Len wiped his eyes and blew his nose, "The death certificate will list the cause of death as cancer. Doc George said not to worry; he'd take care of it."

"I just wish I could have talked to him one more time." Geoff got up and sat back in the chair.

"During your last visit, he was still able to do things, to enjoy your company. That's how you should remember him, as happy and vibrant and loving as he was then. Not what he was at the end."

They both sat back, Geoff letting his mind digest what he'd just been told. Did he blame Len? No, he couldn't. What he'd done was truly humane. Yes, he missed his dad very much, and probably would for some time to come, but for now, they had to get through the next few days of funeral home visits, funerals, and the obligatory grief buffet that would fill the kitchen with green bean casseroles and God knows what else.

"Len, didn't you say we had an appointment at two?"

"Yeah." Len looked tired, really tired.

"Then we should go."

16

Len pushed himself to his feet, and they left the house, getting in Len's truck. Geoff drove while Len rode in silence.

They spent the better part of the next few hours picking out a casket and working through the details of the funeral. The funeral director was so helpful, guiding them through the process. "Do you have anything special you'd like for the service?"

"Yes. Cliff had specifically requested that Geoff give the eulogy at the funeral. He didn't want a minister to do it."

Geoff was floored. Would he be able to give his own father's eulogy?

"Is that what you want, young man?" The funeral director seemed surprised as well.

"Yes." The thought of a stranger or someone who barely knew his dad giving the eulogy at his funeral didn't seem right. "Yes... I'll do it."

Finally, all the arrangements were done, and they drove back to the house. Geoff was surprised to see a car parked by the house, but Len didn't seem to be. Inside, Geoff was pleased to see Aunt Mari, his dad's sister. She hugged him tight and then bustled around the house.

"Sit down, Mari, you're making me nervous," Geoff said.

She plopped herself on the sofa. "Are the arrangements done?"

"Yes. The visitation is tomorrow at six, and the funeral's on Thursday at four."

"Did Cliff have a will?"

Len nodded slowly. "Yes, so there're no issues there. We just need to make it through the next few days."

Geoff stood up, tired of sitting and moping. "Len, come on, let's go for a ride. I think we need to clear our heads." He turned to his aunt. "We'll be back later."

"I'll manage things here." She would, too. Aunt Mari was special. His dad had two other sisters, who were both primo bitches, and they'd show up eventually, but Mari could handle them just fine.

Geoff and Len walked together to the barn, seeing majestic heads peeking out from their stalls. Geoff got treats for each of them, patting noses and saying hello. The last stall was the hardest. That was where Kirkpatrick, his father's horse, was stabled. Geoff patted his nose and gave him a couple of carrots. "You want to go for a ride, boy?" Besides his dad, Geoff was the only other person he'd ever allowed on his back.

"I'll saddle him for you." Geoff turned around and saw one of the grooms standing at the door with Kirk's blanket, saddle, and tack.

"Thank you—"

"Joey," the young man supplied. He stepped forward after setting the blanket and saddle on the top of the stall and started brushing the horse. "He just loves to be brushed." Kirk really seemed to move into Joey's strokes. The groom's movements were practiced and efficient, and soon the horse was groomed, saddled, and ready for their ride.

After thanking the young man, Geoff led Kirk out into the yard as Len was leading his own horse out of the barn.

"Let's ride to the river," Len called, mounting his chestnut gelding. Geoff waved his agreement and mounted his father's jet-black stallion, and they took off around the barn and out across the pasture.

Geoff felt free and light as they rode. As a child, this was where he'd been happiest. In the safety of the pasture, he gave Kirk his head and let him run, the wind whipping his hair and shirt as the powerful animal shot across the pasture. Some of the sorrow from earlier in the day dissipated and his spirit began to soar along with Kirk's.

As they approached the far side of the meadow, he reined the horse in. Kirk began to slow to a canter and finally a walk. "You're such a good boy, you know that?" Geoff patted the horse's neck as he waited for Len.

"That felt good," Geoff said.

"I bet it did." Len was smiling a little as well. "He'd want us to be happy."

"I know; I'm just finding it hard right now."

"Come on. I have something to show you." Len led the way down the wooded trail that led to the river, winding beneath tall trees and around shrubs and brush. When they reached the water, he guided them down a small path for about fifty feet and then stopped, getting off his horse. "This is it."

Geoff looked around. The water was sending sparkles of light across the leaves. "Is this where you and dad—?"

"Yes. This is where he and I had a lot of firsts, and where he and I came to talk when we didn't want little ears to hear." Len looked around. "I can feel him; it's like he's here with me." He shook away his grief and looked at Geoff, a very serious expression on his face. "You have a decision you need to make. Your father put the land, farm, and all of the accounts in both his and your names about five years ago." Geoff started to say something, but Len stopped him. "They are yours now, and you have a decision to make. You could sell them—and they'd bring in a great deal of money—but then they'd be gone, along with your heritage. This land was your great-grandfather's, and now it's yours."

"Is that what you brought me here to tell me?"

"No. I brought you here to tell you that I can tell you're not happy. And don't think for a minute that we both didn't know you were sleeping with every man who came along."

Geoff became indignant. "How…?"

Len silenced him. "I know what that's like because I did it before I met your father. It's hollow, lonely, and deeply unsatisfying, particularly when compared with waking next to someone you love." Geoff's anger deflated as he heard the truth in what Len was saying. "I know you like your job, but does it compare to riding Kirk across the pasture like you just did?" Geoff had the feeling that Len was searching for something in his face. "Your father wanted you to carry on here; he just didn't expect it to be so soon. Neither of us did."

"I don't know what to say."

Len stepped forward, embracing him tightly. "You don't have to say anything now. You just have to decide what it is you really want."

"But I'm an accountant."

Len laughed, really laughed, for the first time since Geoff had arrived. "And this is primarily a business, and a very successful one, I might add." Geoff had never thought of it that way—to him it was just home. "Come on, we need to get back before the vultures start circling your aunt."

"Go on, I'll be along in a minute," Geoff said.

Len mounted and headed back down the trail, leaving Geoff alone with his thoughts. "Well, Kirk, what do you think?" The horse bobbed and shook his head. "Yeah, me too." Geoff remounted, and they walked back to the farm. As soon as they hit the pasture, Kirk took off again, and Geoff urged him on.

They were both breathing heavily when he led Kirk back to his stall. Geoff removed the saddle and brushed the horse down again, making sure he had water and oats before putting the tack away. Joey was in the tack room, cleaning up and making sure everything was in order. "How long have you worked here?" Geoff asked.

Joey turned around, startled. "Um… just a month or so. Len is teaching me how to ride in exchange for working in the barn."

"I'm Geoff." He extended his hand and the younger man took it, "It's good to meet you."

"I'm sorry about your dad. He was a real nice man."

"Thanks. Are you almost done here?"

"Yeah, I was just finishing up."

"Then why don't you come up to the house and have some dinner? I'm sure there's enough for an army."

"Thanks. I just need to finish here first. Len asked me to clean up the tack room."

Geoff remembered that same energy in himself when he was learning to ride and how his own world had revolved around Len.

"Okay, but don't be too long." Geoff walked back to the house, the peace and quiet sinking back into his soul. *Too bad Dad had to die for me to realize how much this place means to me.* Geoff again pushed the grief aside as he climbed the steps to the porch and went inside.

The house was in an uproar. His dad's other two sisters, Janelle and Victoria, had arrived, and they were buzzing through the house. Len was sitting in his chair, obviously tired and definitely overwhelmed. "Geoff!" His Aunt Vicki gave him a dainty hug and then bustled back into the kitchen.

His Aunt Janelle came down the stairs carrying a bag that was obviously quite full. "Geoff." She continued down the stairs, putting the bag by the door before giving him a hug. Len wasn't paying attention, and Geoff saw the look of grief on his face.

"What's in there?" Geoff pointed to the bag by the door.

"Nothing important."

Geoff sighed and walked to the door, picking up the bag and emptying the contents on the sofa. Just as he thought, it was his great-grandmother's quilt. His aunt and his dad had had a running fight over that for as long as he could remember.

He picked up the quilt and handed it to her. "Put it back."

Her eyes widened and then softened into tears. "Your father said that it was—"

Geoff started to smile and then laugh. "Quit the crocodile tears and put it back." He handed it back to her and watched as she marched up the stairs and came down a few minutes later empty-handed. "If you want something, ask, and I'll consider it." She actually opened her mouth to say something and then closed it again.

Without another word, Geoff went into the kitchen and found his Aunt Mari making dinner. "Thank you." He kissed her softly on the cheek.

"How many are there for dinner?" He could see the hope in her eyes.

Geoff smirked. "Four. Joey will be joining us when he's done in the tack room."

"What about them?" She motioned toward where her sisters were sitting in the living room. Geoff shook his head. He needed peace, and so did Len. They were enough to make him sell the farm and send him running back to Chicago with a look of glee on his face. His father had always tolerated his older sisters, but Geoff had never liked them.

Mari smiled and started setting the table, and Geoff went into the living room, his two aunts glaring at him and Len sitting miserable in his chair.

"Len, dinner will be ready in a few minutes." Without waiting for a response, he went to the closet and got his aunts' jackets. "Thank you for coming," He kissed each of them on the cheek. "We'll see you tomorrow." He helped them into their jackets, and they left quietly.

Len sat up and slapped his knee. "God damn it! I've been trying to figure out how to get those bitches to leave for twenty years." Len then settled back in his chair, looking a little more at ease. "You know you haven't heard the last of it."

"I know, but it felt good. She's always...." Geoff could never put his finger on it, but his Aunt Janelle had always seemed false. Oh, she said and did the right things, but there was something cold behind those eyes.

"I used to think she hated us for being gay, but now I'm not so sure. I think it may be that she couldn't stand the fact that Cliff and I found happiness together, 'cause Lord knows, she never could." Len shook his head. "Don't know why your Aunt Vicki puts up with her, but they've always been thick as thieves."

Janelle had never married, and Geoff thought it was because no one could stand her that long. But his Aunt Vicki was generally a sweet person, and as long as Janelle wasn't around, she was wonderful. However, the minute Janelle showed up, Vicki turned

Andrew Grey

into a bitch. He couldn't help wondering how Uncle Dan and his two cousins, Jill and Christopher, could stand it.

Joey came in a few minutes later, breaking him out of thoughts about his family, thank God, and they washed up and got ready for dinner, talking about horses and everything else but Geoff's dad as they ate.

Len commented between bites, "So it sounds like you've decided." Geoff looked across the table, and he could swear on a stack of bibles that he saw Len smirk like he'd known it all the time.

"Yes." Geoff got up and carried his dishes to the sink. "I'm moving back here. This is home."

CHAPTER 3

TWO weeks later, Geoff had loaded all his things into the back of a truck he'd brought from the farm. Thank God it hadn't rained. His father's funeral had gone well, with a lot of tears and even more reminiscing and wandering down memory lane. Geoff had indeed given the eulogy and found he'd reduced most of the people in the church to tears. Thankfully, he'd managed to stave off his own until he was done speaking. Then he'd taken his seat next to Len and cried on his shoulder.

A few days later, he'd returned to Chicago to resign from his employment and empty out his apartment. Mr. Vain had been surprised and even hinted that he'd like to get together with Geoff again, but Geoff dismissed him offhand and spent the better part of the last two weeks turning his work over to others.

Raine had been disappointed that Geoff was leaving, but he'd taken it in stride.

"You could always come with me," Geoff said.

Raine had scoffed, "What am I going to do on a farm?" Then they'd both laughed and arranged to go for a drink one last time before Geoff left town. They'd had a good friendship, and Geoff made Raine promise he'd come for a visit.

The drive back to the farm was pleasant, and Geoff rode contentedly, the windows open and music on the radio. He arrived just before noon and pulled in the drive. The house was quiet with Len out working, so Geoff unloaded what he could, figuring they could get the rest later. When Len arrived, Geoff had lunch ready and waiting.

"What are you doing the rest of the day?" Len quizzed as he sat down.

"Unloading the truck and then working with the horses. I want to get that stall ready for Princess; she should be just about ready to foal, unless she did it while I was gone."

"Nope, she looks like she'll be ready in the next few days. The boys and I'll be in the west pasture riding fences. I want to move a hundred head in there." They sat down and started eating. "How did it go with your job and this Raine?"

"The job was easy enough, but Raine was much harder to leave. He's the best friend I've had in a long time." Geoff continued eating quickly; he had plenty to do and wanted to get it done. "Tonight I thought I'd look at the books, get familiar with them." Before he left he'd learned that the farm employed three men full time and a few part-timers who helped with general chores, like cleaning stalls and bringing in hay.

"Could you do that tomorrow? I have something I need to talk to you about tonight," Len requested.

"Sure." Geoff took his and Len's dishes to the sink. "I'll get those later."

Geoff went back outside to finish unloading the truck. Once he had everything inside, he drove the truck to the barn and got to work preparing the largest stall for the impending birth. Once he was done, he cleaned out a few other stalls, watered all the horses, and filled their mangers with hay and some oats. Joey arrived as he was finishing up and brought more hay from the loft and swept the barn floor.

"Join us for dinner, Joey?"

"I can't tonight. Mom's planning a special dinner for my birthday." He seemed so excited.

"Then get home and start celebrating!" Geoff scooted him out of the barn and watched as he ran to his bike and took off home. Len and the men were all heading toward the house, and Geoff wondered what was going on until he remembered it was Friday, the night of Len's weekly poker game.

The weekly poker game had been a tradition on the farm... forever. Geoff could remember as a kid sitting next to Len, watching him play, learning from him the entire time.

"Geoffy... you gonna come and get your ass whupped at cards?" one of the men called out.

"I'll be in soon!" he called back, smiling. Fred had always called him Geoffy—he was the only person on Earth who got away with it. It was nice to be home. The city had been fun, but these people cared about him, had known him most of his life.

But things were different now. Before, his dad had been the boss. He was the one making the tough decisions, and Geoff hadn't really been involved and hadn't had to worry about the consequences. Now, Geoff was the boss, and everyone on the farm was going to look to him to make decisions.

It made him nervous. Granted, he had Len for advice and help, but the farm, the animals, and the people who worked there depended on it for their livelihood; they were his responsibility now.

"Jesus, what am I going to do?" The enormity of what he'd taken on hit him all at once. He leaned against the side of the barn and forced breath into his lungs. "Take it one step at a time. That's what dad would say." He took another deep breath, "Fuck and Christ, now I'm talking to myself. Get your head on straight and don't be a baby. You grew up here. You know what to do." The sense of panic started to subside, and he breathed easier.

Getting himself together, he stepped into the barn and headed for Kirk's stall. The majestic black head poked out of the stall as soon as he got close. Geoff got a carrot and fed it to Kirk, rubbing his nose, the horse calming the last of his nerves as it munched loudly, those huge, deep eyes watching him closely. "You are something else, boy."

Len had tried to convince his dad for years to have Kirk gelded, but Cliff would have none of it, and Geoff had no intention of doing it either. With a farewell stroke of that black nose, Geoff left the barn and headed toward the house.

The kitchen was filled with voices and laughter, the four men talking and joking easily with each other.

"Come on, Geoffy, pull up a chair."

He took a seat away from Fred, and Len dealt him in the next hand. Simon continued the banter. "Pete, did you see Joey brushing Kirk this afternoon?" Kirk wouldn't let Pete get anywhere near him without trying to bite the short, stocky man. Not that he'd let Simon, a.k.a. Lumpy, anywhere near him either, but Pete had always bragged about how good he was with horses.

A cheese curl went flying across the table. "Knock it off, Lumpy." The aim was good—it left an orange splotch on Simon's shirt.

"Are we gonna play?" Pete grumbled into his cards.

They settled down as the betting got under way. Not that there was big money involved. Geoff thought that someone might have won five dollars once, years ago. For them, it was all about who could bluff whom.

Geoff couldn't help himself and got in on the ribbing, "Come on, guys, Kirk's a big baby."

Fred snickered. "Only 'cause he likes you."

"And apparently Joey." The fact that the teenager found favor with the stallion amused Geoff immensely. Geoff always felt that horses could sense what was in your heart, and Kirk was a particularly astute horse. That he liked Joey spoke a lot about the young man, as far as Geoff was concerned. It didn't hurt that the kid was as cute as they came, either. If he were a little older.... Geoff had to force the thought from his mind as he bet carefully with his full house.

Sure enough, Lumpy bet big, which meant he was probably bluffing, and Geoff called him.

"Three nines." The tall, wiry man laid down his cards, grinning like a cat.

Geoff smiled and showed his cards. "Full house." Lumpy groaned and threw in his cards while Geoff raked in the pot. "Joey seems like a real good kid," Geoff commented, and the conversation around the table stopped. "What?" He hadn't expected the simple comment to have such an effect.

Len leaned forward, voice low and serious. "His daddy died a year ago, and his mom's doing her best, but it ain't easy for her.

Joey'd been hanging around the barn for a while, and he finally asked how much riding lessons cost. I told him if he'd help around the barn, I'd give him lessons for free. You should have seen his face—lit up like a Christmas tree. That look alone was worth a year of lessons." Somehow Geoff didn't doubt it. "Why, what are you thinking?" Len somehow could tell an idea was percolating, but Geoff shook his head, not ready to talk about it yet.

Geoff patted Len on the shoulder. "You old softie," he accused as he went to the refrigerator. "Anybody need anything?" The conversation around the table returned to normal.

"I'll take a beer." Geoff got two and handed one to Len before sitting back down.

Fred picked up the cards and started shuffling as antes were thrown in. "I hear your Aunt Janelle's mad enough to spit nails at you." Pete was dating Geoff's cousin Jill. They were pretty serious, and whatever Janelle felt, Vicki and her kids were gonna hear about it.

Len muttered something—sounded like "old witch"—but Geoff took it in stride. "She tried to steal something from the house when she was visiting after dad died. I caught her and made her put it back, so of course she's mad." *Conniving woman.*

Fred piped in, "You know that woman's the most vindictive creature ever put on this Earth." The cards were dealt and the hand began.

"Don't really care. She can go be vindictive someplace else. She's not gonna steal from me and get away with it. Hell, she's lucky I didn't let her leave and then call the police." Geoff decided it was time to change the subject, "So Pete, how are you Jilly getting along?" Bets were thrown into the pot while they talked.

Pete immediately turned red. The youngest of the group, apart from Geoff, he'd had a crush on Jill since high school. Two years earlier, he'd finally worked up the nerve to ask her on a date. They'd been inseparable since. "We're doing good."

Fred supplied the details. "Pete's gonna ask her to marry him as soon as he can afford the ring."

Pete still looked embarrassed,. "I'm almost there."

Geoff smiled at Pete. "Good for you. She's a nice girl who deserves someone who'll be good to her." His cousin *was* nice, not particularly bright, but down-to-earth, very sweet, and nurturing. There was no doubt they'd take good care of each other and make good parents.

"What does it feel like to be the Boss-man?" Lumpy could usually be counted on to be a pain in the ass.

Geoff thought quickly about how to answer. "Don't know yet; we'll see what it feels like when I sign your paycheck." A chorus of "Ooooos" came from around the table, and then everyone laughed. He'd known these guys for some time; none of them were strangers, but he could see and feel that things had changed slightly. They used to pick on him and tease him. Now, other than Fred, that was largely absent. Geoff knew why and knew it was inevitable; he just wasn't sure how he felt about it.

Geoff folded and threw in his cards, watching the remainder of the hand as the comfortable conversation and easy ribbing the guys gave one another continued around the table. Rumors and gossip were shared.

"Lumpy, did you hear that old man Jones claims he saw a bear on his property?" Len asked.

Lumpy laughed. "Like he claimed he saw a gorilla two years ago that turned out to be a combination of a scarecrow and too much whiskey."

All the guys laughed except Len. "Just the same, be on the lookout for any signs."

"There hasn't been a bear in the county in twenty years. I bet it was one of the Hamms' bears he saw through the bottom of his beer glass," Lumpy said.

The card game broke up about nine, as it usually did. The guys helped to clean up and then hit the road. Most of them lived within a couple miles of the farm.

"Len, did you know today was Joey's birthday?" Geoff asked. Len's reply was a shake of his head. "I saw him at the barn today wearing old tennis shoes and jeans with more patches than denim," Geoff added.

"What are you getting at?" Len glared at him, "You don't want him around anymore; is that it?" The glare turned into a scowl. "'Cause I raised you better than that."

"Don't get your underwear in a twist." What had Len so growly all of a sudden? "I was thinking that tomorrow I'd take him in to town, and we'd get him a birthday present. I was thinking a pair of boots, a proper pair of jeans, and maybe a hat. If he's gonna be out in the sun, he'll need one."

Len turned away, and Geoff knew he was trying to hide the fact that he was feeling emotional. "Sometimes I forget just how much of your father there is in you."

"There's just as much of you in me as there is him. Remember that." Geoff patted Len's shoulder and then went into what had been his father's office to give Len some privacy. He looked around and found the ledgers and records on the desk and started looking through them. It became apparent that they weren't up to date, which wasn't a surprise, and he sat down at the desk and got to work.

An hour later, he'd been able to map out what his dad had been doing and what needed to be done to get the books caught up. He also made a note to go down to the bank to talk to them about the farm accounts, find out about his dad's personal accounts, and see what was going on with something his father listed as his emergency account.

Len knocked on the door frame. "Can we talk for a while?"

Geoff closed the ledgers and turned off the light. "Living room?" Len nodded, and Geoff got up and followed him.

Len sat in his usual chair. "I've decided that I'm going to move."

"What? Where are you going?" This was not good. He didn't want Len going anywhere.

"Sorry... I mean that I want to change bedrooms. The house is yours, and you should be using the master bedroom, and...." Geoff waited for him to finish. "Sleeping in that room without Cliff... I thought I could do it, but I just can't. There're too many memories," Len finished.

Geoff wasn't sure he could use the room either, but he could understand Len's feelings. "I'll help you move whenever you want."

"Thank you." Len reached into his pocket and pulled out an envelope. "Your dad asked me to give this to you once you'd made your decision about keeping the farm." Len handed it to him and got out of the chair. "I'll see you in the morning." He then went upstairs.

Geoff stared at the envelope he held in his hand. He could see his name on it in his dad's distinctive scrawl. Finally, he opened it and pulled out a handwritten letter.

Andrew Grey

My Darling Son:

By now I'm sure that Len has told you what I did and why. I know you're probably upset with me, but this is what I wanted. These last few months have been filled with unending pain from the cancer and prodding from the doctors. I'm sorry I didn't tell you, but I know you would have tried to talk me out of it, and I could never deny you anything.

I asked Len to give you this letter once you'd made a decision about keeping or selling the farm. In case you're wondering, I know what you chose, and I'm proud you decided to keep it. You will be the fourth generation to run the farm, and I know you'll pass it on to the next generation in as good a shape as I'm passing it to you. You love this land as much as I do; it's in your blood.

There are some things I need you to do. Please take care of Len. He's the love of my life, and I was blessed with both him and you. I hope he'll find someone and be happy again, and you mustn't try to stop him. He deserves all the happiness he can find in this world, just as you do. Farming can be a very lonely life, so find yourself someone to love who loves you back. That makes everything else worth it.

Finally, I want to tell you how much I love you and how proud I am to have you as a son.

You brightened my life every day. The first time
I held you, I couldn't fathom how quickly
anyone could capture my heart, but one look
from your big blue eyes, and I was a goner. As
you grew up, you became an extraordinary
man with a huge capacity for love and caring.
You will be tried by many things in the years to
come, but whatever happens, remain the same
loving, caring person you are today.

I love you always,

Dad

Geoff's eyes stung and his throat hurt as he finished the letter
and put it back in the envelope. Walking back into the office, he
placed the letter in the top drawer, turned off the lights, and went
upstairs, his father's words singing in his ears.

Andrew Grey

CHAPTER 4

GEOFF had never needed an alarm to get him up in the morning—
well, at least when he hadn't been drinking—and this morning
wasn't an exception. It was still dark, and Geoff was out of bed,
cleaned up, dressed, and in the kitchen grabbing a bite to eat before
going to the barn for his morning ride. He heard a soft knock and
opened the door to find Lumpy standing on the steps, looking
concerned. "There's something in the barn that you have to see."

Geoff felt dubious but followed Lumpy across the yard, into
the barn, and down to the empty stall on the end, where he saw a
pair of black boots. Looking into the stall, he was surprised to see a
pair of legs, and peeking around the corner, the sleeping form of
what looked like a boy. The barn was still largely dark, with only the
early morning light coming through the windows and open door, but
it was enough for Geoff to see that this boy was extraordinary. It
was only after seeing his sleeping face that he noticed the black
pants sticking out from under the black coat he was using as a
blanket, and the wide-brimmed black hat that had been carefully set
on the empty manger. What on earth was an Amish boy doing
sleeping in his barn?

Geoff didn't get much time to contemplate the question, because a few seconds later, the boy's eyes opened and immediately filled with fear. Suddenly he was on his feet and running like a jackrabbit out of the barn and into the yard. Lumpy looked at Geoff and took off after him, but Geoff called him back. "I'll go. You get started with your work." Lumpy nodded, and Geoff picked up the hat and pair of boots, walking outside. Dawn was just starting to break, and he could see the boy standing by the road, looking back at the barn.

Geoff walked slowly in his direction, treating the boy like a spooked horse, making no sudden movements. "You forgot your boots and hat." Geoff held them out to him, and when the boy didn't move forward, Geoff slowly bent down and set them on the ground. "It's okay, I won't hurt you." He stepped back, and the boy moved forward, pulling on his boots and taking his hat. "Why were you sleeping in the barn? Where's your family?"

"*Rumspringa.*"

The word sounded foreign to Geoff. "I don't know what that means."

The young man—Geoff could see now that he was definitely not a boy—stood back up again, those intense blue eyes boring into him. "It is my time away from the community."

Geoff nodded, not really understanding too much about Amish life other than what he'd heard secondhand. But if the boy was supposed to live away from the community and he was sleeping in his barn, he obviously didn't have a place to stay. "Are you hungry?"

The young man stood stock still as if deciding whether to answer or bolt, to listen to his fear or his stomach. "Yes."

Geoff smiled and extended his hand. "I'm Geoff, and this is my farm."

37

The Amish youth looked around, his eyes traveling over the house and barns, his expression filling with awe. "I'm Elijah, Elijah Henninger." He took Geoff's hand and shook it tentatively.

"All right, Elijah, follow me, and we'll get you some breakfast." Geoff turned and walked toward the house, checking to see if Elijah was following. "It's okay. We're just going inside." He led them to the back door and into the kitchen. Elijah followed and immediately took off his hat when he came inside, unsure of where to go or what to do.

The look of surprise on Len's face when he saw the young Amish man standing in the kitchen was hard to miss, but luckily Elijah was looking around and didn't see it. Geoff pretended he hadn't seen it either and started talking as though there was nothing out of the ordinary. "Is breakfast almost ready?"

For a second, Len looked at him like he had three heads, but then he remembered his manners. "About ten minutes."

"Good." Geoff motioned Elijah over. "Len, this is Elijah; he'll be joining us for breakfast. Elijah, this is Leonard—Len. He's the foreman here on the farm." There was no way that Geoff was going to try to explain their relationship, and Len seemed to understand and followed his lead.

Geoff indicated a chair, and Elijah sat down, placing his hat beneath the chair. "Thank you, sir."

Len finished dishing up the food, putting three plates at their places on the table while Geoff poured glasses of juice and set them at each place.

"What's that?" Geoff saw Elijah pointing at the glass.

Oh my God… what a realization. "It's orange juice; try it." Elijah looked dubious but took a sip and smiled, tasting some more before putting the glass back down. He then started eating with gusto, the eggs, pancakes, and toasted bread disappearing quickly, washed down by the juice. He was definitely hungry. Geoff watched out of the corner of his eye as he ate his own breakfast and sipped his coffee. He'd poured Elijah a cup, and the young man had sipped it, shuddered, and put the cup back down, not touching it again.

Len had been watching Elijah with a strange look on his face. "I know you." Then he remembered. "I see you at the bakery when I buy bread."

A banging outside startled all of them, with Elijah jumping a little in his chair, and then Fred hurried into in the kitchen, his eyes widening when he saw Elijah. "Len, it's Princess; she's struggling with the foal. I called the vet, but she's on another call. Her office said she'd be here as soon as she can."

"Fuck and damn." Len leapt from his chair, grabbed his coat, and was out the door with Fred right behind him.

Geoff gulped the last of his coffee like he was downing a shot of whiskey and grabbed his coat as well. He wasn't sure what he could do, but he was sure as hell not going to sit here while one of his horses was in trouble. "Come on!" He handed Elijah his coat and rushed out the door, Elijah following on his heels.

"Do you know about birthing horses?" Elijah called from behind him.

He'd seen it plenty of times, and he knew what was supposed to happen, but Geoff had never helped with a birth, and he'd never seen a troubled one. He called over his shoulder, "Not really." They arrived in the barn to some very agitated horses. Geoff turned to the men standing around Princess's stall. "Get the rest of these horses turned out."

The men snapped to and started opening stalls, getting halters on horses and leading them out of the barn. Slowly, the barn started to quiet, and Geoff looked into Princess's stall. His heart nearly broke. She was lying on her side, covered in sweat, breathing like she'd just won a race, head thrashing, and her eyes… begging for help. Geoff stepped back and bumped into Elijah. "Sorry." He hoped to hell the vet got here soon.

Elijah looked into the stall, and Geoff stood aside. Elijah watched for a moment before turning back to Geoff, handing him his coat and hat, and rolling up his sleeves. Saying nothing more, he stepped into the stall, speaking soft and low to the agitated horse while he felt her belly. "The foal's in the wrong position. It's not too bad, but it needs to be turned." He stood back up. "Where can I wash?"

Geoff indicated the bathroom near the tack room and watched as Elijah walked inside. Water ran, and then Elijah emerged wearing his undershirt, walking straight into Princess's stall.

Geoff was amazed at the transformation. Gone was the tentative boy who'd bolted that morning as soon as he'd seen them, and in his place was a tall, confident young man who seemed to know what to do and had the confidence to do it.

Elijah began speaking softly, his voice soothing as he felt the mare's stomach again. "I'll need some help." Geoff and Len joined him in the stall, waiting for instructions. "I'm going to try to turn the foal. I need you to keep her as calm as you can."

Geoff sat near Princess's head, stroking her neck and soothing her with his voice as he watched what Elijah was doing. Len knelt near her back, stroking her and likewise doing his best to keep her calm.

Elijah positioned himself behind Princess and slowly inserted first one hand and then the other. The horse started to move, but Geoff was able to soothe her back down. "I almost have it; just keep her still." Princess twitched like she was trying to get up, and Geoff and Len did their best to calm her, trying to keep her still. Then he saw Elijah slide his hands free and step back.

A minute later, a small hoof appeared and then another, followed by a head, shoulders, and then—whoosh—the rest of the foal followed. Elijah stood back as Len took over, making sure everything was okay and getting the foal away so Princess could stand, which she did right away. Then Len, too, vacated the stall, and everyone watched as the little colt rested on the straw. In a few minutes, he extended his legs and tried to stand. After a few tries, he was up on wobbly legs; then he was down and up again. This time, he managed a few tentative steps toward his mother and started to suckle.

Everyone in the barn breathed a collective sigh of relief, with the men smiling and patting Elijah on the back. Elijah just grinned and went into the bathroom to clean up.

The barn door opened and closed, and Geoff saw Jane Grove, the vet, hurrying in his direction.

"Where's Princess?" she asked.

Geoff pointed to the stall and watched as the doctor opened the door and stopped cold. The last thing she could have expected to see was a suckling colt standing in the stall. "I thought there was a problem."

"There was. The colt was in the wrong position and needed to be turned."

"Who did it?" She looked at each of the men. The bathroom door opened, and Elijah stepped out, walking to Geoff, who handed him his coat and hat.

"Elijah did."

She smiled. "How'd you know what to do?"

He looked at Geoff and seemed unsure of what to do. Finally, he answered, speaking to Geoff, "One of Papa's horses had the same problem about a year ago, and I helped Papa turn the foal. He told me what to do and what to look for."

"I'm going to check them both over just in case." She went into the stall, and Len stayed with her while Geoff and Elijah left the barn.

"Thank you. By the time Jane got here, it would probably have been too late, and we would have lost either Princess or her foal. I owe you a debt."

Elijah's face registered surprise that changed into a bright smile. "You owe me nothing." He put on his coat and hat and started walking toward the road.

"Where are you going?"

Elijah shrugged. "It's my year away from the community, so I have to make my way in the outside world."

"Would you like a job?" Geoff told himself that Elijah had skills the farm could use; he knew his way around animals and wasn't afraid of farm work. Geoff had no doubt Elijah could make a contribution. "I need another man who can help around here, and you need to make your way in the world. Could you do that here?"

Elijah looked extremely conflicted. "Are you serious? Live among the English?"

Geoff didn't understand the last part. "Yes, I'm serious, and I'm not English."

Elijah laughed. "English is what we call outsiders, people who aren't Amish."

"Oh." Geoff smiled. He couldn't help it; Elijah's smile was bright and catching. The man was beautiful when he smiled. Geoff wanted to smack himself for having those thoughts and forced his mind back to business. "Well, do you want to work here... among the English?" The term tickled him for some reason.

Elijah looked around the farm; it obviously intrigued him. "Okay."

Geoff was pleased. "Then let's find you a place to stay." Geoff led the way into the house and up the stairs. The old farmhouse had four bedrooms, and Geoff opened the door to the one farthest away from him and Len, figuring it would give Elijah some privacy. It was also the room his father had used as a guest room, so it had its own small bathroom, which might be easier on Elijah. The room was small and plain, containing little but the bed and dresser Geoff had used when he lived in Chicago.

"You want me to stay here in your house?"

Geoff didn't know how to respond to that. They didn't have a bunkhouse; the guys either had their own places or lived with their families, so they'd never needed one. "You can't live in the barn, and if you're going to work here, you need a place to stay."

"I guess... I just don't want to be a bother."

Geoff shook his head. "It's just Len and me in this big house. There's plenty of room." He showed Elijah where the bathroom was and then led the way back downstairs and into the kitchen, where he started making coffee. Len came in as he was finishing up. "That was really something to watch."

"It was. Elijah knew exactly what to do."

"Where is he?"

Geoff looked around and spotted a slight movement. "In the living room. I hired him on this morning." Len's eyes went wide. "He's on his year away from the community, and he needs to make his own way. Lord knows we could use the help around here, and he knows his way around a farm." Len looked at Geoff strangely but said nothing. "I gave him the room at the far end of the hall," Geoff said.

"He'll need some clothes; he's probably only got what he's wearing," Len said.

"I was gonna take Joey into town to get his birthday present. I'll see if Elijah wants to go along as well." Geoff went in search of Elijah, finding him on the front porch, dogs all around him getting scratches and loving, crawling over one another to get closer.

Elijah was laughing something fierce, his face getting licked and kissed from all sides.

Geoff called the dogs away. "Come on, guys. He'll be around for a while."

Elijah got up and walked inside, still smiling and happy. He sat in the same chair he had for breakfast while the others helped themselves to coffee.

"You work at the bakery, don't you?" Les asked.

"Yes, sir. I work with my uncle when he needs help, mostly on Saturday when he's real busy."

Len nodded. "I thought you looked familiar."

Elijah looked at the table. "I'm sorry I don't remember you, sir." It looked to Geoff as though he were going to say something more but stopped himself.

"I wouldn't expect you would." Len said.

Geoff finished his coffee quickly and put his mug in the sink. "I'm going into town this afternoon and was wondering if you'd like to go along. You'll need some other clothes to work in."

Elijah looked down at himself. "I don't have much money, certainly not enough for store-bought clothes."

"Don't worry about it."

Elijah's head shot up. "No! I can't have you buying me things. It wouldn't be right."

"Then you can work them off." The fire in Elijah's eyes died down slightly as Geoff answered. "I'll buy the clothes and take the cost out of your pay." Geoff could understand not wanting to be beholden to anyone, particularly a stranger. "Okay?"

Elijah nodded; that seemed to make him happy.

They heard a knock on the back door, and Len answered it, returning with Joey behind him, carrying a plate wrapped in foil. "Lumpy said you wanted to see me," Joey said. He put the plate on the counter. "Mom sent over some cake."

"Joey, I know that yesterday was your birthday, so as a birthday present I'm going to take you into town. Len says that you're becoming quite a horseman, so it's time you looked the part. You need boots, a hat, and some riding jeans. Is that okay?" The look he got from the boy was pure, unexpected, speechless joy. Geoff smiled in return. "Be ready to go in half an hour." Joey nodded, still smiling, and left the kitchen. Len and Geoff watched him running across the yard to the barn.

Len finished his coffee and started washing out the mugs as he asked, "Are you going into Ludington or Scottville?" The farm was located between the two towns. "We need a few things from the hardware store, if you're going to Scottville."

"Then Scottville it is."

Len reached into his pocket and pulled out his list and handed it to Geoff, his face long and sad.

"Are you okay?"

"I will be. I just miss him."

Geoff nodded and left Len with his thoughts.

Geoff found Elijah back on the front porch playing with the pups, and he stood up as soon as he saw his new employer. "Do you buy birthday presents for everyone who works here?"

"No." Geoff was initially confused by the question. "Oh… Joey's dad died a year ago, and his mom's been having a tough time of it."

Elijah thought for a few minutes. "So you're using his birthday as an excuse to buy him the things he needs without making him feel bad?"

"Sort of, I guess." Geoff tried to think of a way he could help Elijah understand. "In your community, when someone needs something, everyone helps them out, right?" Elijah nodded. "Think of this farm sort of like that. Joey needs things, and he works hard for us. Len and I getting them for him will make him happy and help him out at the same time."

"Papa always said that the English don't do something for nothing."

Geoff wasn't surprised. Most people had misconceptions about people different from themselves. "Sometimes happiness is its own reward. The look on Joey's face when I told him was worth a lot more than money."

Walking out to the yard, they found Joey in the barn laying straw in a clean stall. "You ready?" Geoff asked. Joey nodded as he broke open a last bale of straw before spreading it on the floor.

"All set." Joey's excitement was evident in his walk as they headed to the truck. The three of them got in, with Joey in the middle and Elijah by the door, and as they pulled out, Geoff saw Elijah grab onto the handle above his head. "Joey, this is Elijah. He'll be working on the farm.

"Hi, Eli." They shook hands, Elijah with the one wasn't using to hang on. "I'm Joey. It's nice to meet you." Geoff had expected Elijah to balk at being called Eli, but Elijah said nothing about it.

They rode down country roads toward the small farming community of Scottville. Geoff parked along Main Street in front of the dry-goods store, and they got out of the truck, Eli looking a little peaked. "You okay, Eli?" Joey grabbed Eli's arm until he was steady on his feet.

Eli stood still and his color started to come back, "I'm not used to riding in cars, I guess. Papa would never allow it. When Mama was sick, he insisted on taking her to the doctor in the buggy, even when the farmer up the road offered to drive them." That seemed shortsighted and a little stubborn to Geoff, but he said nothing. Eli's father obviously had strong beliefs and didn't believe in compromising them.

"Let's go in." Geoff led them into the store and downstairs to the clothing section. "Eli, pick out what you think you'll need." Eli nodded and looked through the clothes as Geoff took Joey to the shoe area. He tried on boots until they figured out his size, and Joey chose a pair of black harness boots. Then they found a cowboy hat that fit and a pair of boot-cut jeans. Joey was grinning, holding his presents like they were solid gold as Geoff searched for Eli.

He found him standing in front of a display of jeans, staring. He didn't look away as Geoff approached. "I always wanted a pair of these, but I knew Papa would never allow it, so I never asked."

Geoff reached to the display and pulled out a pair that he thought might be Eli's size, "Try these on to see if they fit." Eli looked at him like he was kidding. "These are the best type of pants to wear on the farm; they last and protect your legs." Geoff pointed him to the dressing room, and Eli slowly went inside like things were just too good to be true. A few minutes later, he stepped out. Geoff had been right; the jeans were Eli's size. "You'll probably need three pairs for now and some shirts as well."

Eli picked out the plainest jeans and three dark, solid-color shirts. Geoff had him get another pair of shoes and some underclothes. Geoff asked if he wanted another hat, but Eli had said that he'd use the one he had. Chuckling to himself, he led Eli and Joey to the register.

"Geoff, it's Ginny, Ginny Rogers."

"Oh, hey, Ginny." He remembered her now from high school "It's been awhile." She was homely back then, but she'd grown up pretty.

"It has. Is all this yours?" She gave him a huge smile way too big for a casual encounter. He was being flirted with a little. He almost said she was barking up the wrong tree but held his tongue.

"This is Joey and Eli." He gave her his best smile. "Guys, this is Ginny. I went to school with her." She got busy ringing them up; then he handed her his credit card and signed the receipt, Ginny smiling and wiggling the entire time.

She bagged up everything, calling out "Don't be a stranger," waving and flashing her brightest smile as they walked upstairs toward the front door… and right into his Aunt Janelle.

"Geoff." She tried to sound pleased, but it was way too forced.

"Morning, Aunt Janelle." Geoff was determined to kill her with kindness, because that was all she was ever getting from him.

Her eyes raked over Joey and Eli, widening visibly when she saw Eli's clothes.

Quietly, Geoff instructed them, "Go wait in the truck. I'll be out in a minute." There was no way he was subjecting them to her venom or whatever it was that had her panties in a twist.

Her eyes were dark. "Corrupting the Amish?" If she were a man, Geoff would have decked her right there in the store. "Your father and Len living together was bad enough, and I'd hoped somehow you would turn out normal anyway. But corrupting children...."

So that was her problem. He'd always thought that was part of it, but to be so cruel.... Geoff got himself under control before he said something he'd regret. "You listen here. Len and my father loved each other, which is something you'd never understand. So I suggest you keep your poison and your distorted ideas about them to yourself."

She tried to look like the injured party for the few people in the store, but it wasn't working. The people in town knew how she was and gave Geoff sympathetic looks.

"I don't know what you want, because a quilt certainly isn't worth this much effort, but let me tell you this, you won't get it," Geoff promised.

She tried to look revolted. "I don't want anything from you."

"Good, then give me your key. I know you've had a key to the house for years. Now, give it to me."

She started to sputter. "I grew up in that house. You can't—"

"I most certainly can. It's my house and my farm." He held out his hand and waited. She sputtered and spluttered and finally dug into her purse and pulled out her key ring. After fumbling around, she finally handed him the key. Without saying anything else, he turned around, left the store, and got in the truck, putting his head on the steering wheel.

"That is one evil woman."

"That she is, Eli... that she is." Geoff sat back and started the truck, heading to the hardware store as he tried to put his aunt out of his mind. It didn't take him long to get the things Len needed. "Are you two up for The Dairy Barn?" Their smiles were all the answer he needed, quickly dispelling the remnants of Aunt Janelle's venom.

CHAPTER 5

THE next few weeks were busy—very busy—particularly for Geoff as he tried to bring the farm business accounts as well as the livestock records up to date. On top of that, early May was a busy time in general with planting just around the corner. And as he reviewed all the records, Geoff was surprised at just how much planting they did.

He was sitting in the office going over some records when he came across the deeds for the farm and other land. It seemed that a number of years earlier, Geoff's father had purchased a lot of farmland when the market was low and just held onto it. In order to help diversify the business, he'd started planting that acreage in corn and alfalfa for livestock feed and selling what he didn't need.

"Jesus Christ." He looked at the numbers again, blinking in disbelief; that decision had been a good one, really good. They made half their profits from the excess grain, and it diversified the farm so they weren't reliant on one single source of income. "Go Dad."

"What was that?" Len stuck his head in the office on his way to the kitchen to get a snack.

"Nothing, just looking over the records, getting everything up to date, wondering if I can do the job my dad did." Doubt still crept up on Geoff every once in a while.

Len leaned against the door frame. He hadn't actually ever come into the office. Leaning on the frame was as close as he'd come. "Your father was brilliant at being able to spot a bargain and making it pay, there's no doubt about that. This farm was a quarter the size it is now when he inherited it. But don't let that get to you, not at all. He didn't have your knack with the horses, and he certainly didn't get along with the hands as well as you do. I had to be a buffer, or they'd all'a quit."

"Thanks, Len. Sometimes I just think I've taken on too much. There's a lot riding on the decisions I make, and I don't want to get things wrong."

"I'm here; Fred, Lumpy, and Pete are here; and we care about this place as much as you do. We've all put our blood, sweat, and tears into this place, so we're here for you. We'll help, and we'll tell you if we think something's wrong."

Geoff noticed Len watching him for a while. "What is it that's really gotten to you?" Len asked.

"I just can't figure out how we'll get all this land tilled, planted, and ready in time."

"There's your problem; we don't till. In the fall we harvest and leave the remains in the fields. Most of it breaks down over the winter, and in the spring we just plant again. That helps the soil and prevents erosion of the topsoil. Provided it doesn't rain, we'll start planting in the next couple of weeks. I've already got Lumpy tuning up the equipment and getting everything ready."

Geoff got up from the desk and walked to Len, putting his arms around his neck and giving the man a hug. "Thanks."

"There's nothing to be scared of. I got your back." Len returned the hug like he always did. "While you were growing up, I was always careful what I called you, didn't want you to get confused. Cliff was your dad, and you were his son. So I always called you Geoff, and you always called me Len. But I always thought of you as my son."

"I may have called you Len, but I always thought of you as my dad just as much as him." It was starting again. Geoff could feel his grief welling up again. "Good God, we're turning into girls."

They both laughed and released the hug. That had become their catchphrase whenever they were getting really maudlin. Geoff wiped his eyes and went back to the desk. There were some questions he wanted to ask, but the phone rang, distracting him. "Hello."

"Geoff, is that you? Ready to come back to the city?" That voice just rang through the line.

"Raine, how are you? It's good to hear from you again. I called, but you must have been out." Geoff closed the ledgers and books, putting things away while he talked.

"Yeah, I got your message. I was at Spank. God, was that place hopping. Bet you miss the nightlife." He could almost see Raine dancing at Spank, having a good time.

"Don't really have time to miss it. Way too busy with planning, the accounts, learning everything my dad did around here. But I go riding every day, and the guys are really cool, and I've met some people I went to high school with."

"Sounds dreary, but then again, so is the office now that you're gone."

"You were talking about leaving the company before I left," Geoff reminded him.

"I'm looking. Mr. Vain certainly isn't making this place any more fun, that's for sure. Everything is about making him look good, and that man is *dumb*." Raine made all kinds of sounds to illustrate just how dumb he was, and that started Geoff laughing. It felt good to laugh, really laugh. "So I gotta ask, have you met any hot country boys? Like you see on calendars and stuff."

Geoff snickered. "No. I haven't met any boys at all, not really. The only guys are the ones who work for me, and most of them are married. Besides, I've been too busy." He really had. His days started early, and he was exhausted by the time he went to bed.

"You said most of the guys are married. What about the other ones?" Raine *would* pick up on that.

Geoff heard the television click on in the living room: Len watching some sitcom, the laughter carrying into the office. "Jesus, Raine, you want me to rob the cradle or something?"

"What about the guy you found sleeping in the barn? He didn't sound too young."

"Eli?"

"He's over eighteen, isn't he? Is he cute?" Geoff was about to answer when something clicked in his brain. Eli *was* cute… in fact, Eli was…. He pulled his mind away from that thought. There was no way he was thinking about Eli like that.

"Well?" Raine asked persistently.

Geoff just couldn't go there. "Eli's Amish, Raine." He tried to make the very idea sound ridiculous so Raine would drop it.

"You mean *Amish* Amish, like they-use-horse-and-buggies Amish?" Geoff laughed; he couldn't help it. The disbelief in Raine's voice was completely priceless. To someone like Raine, who couldn't get along without his cell phone, microwave oven, video games, and every other electronic device known to man, the thought of going without any of it must have sounded like a stint in pure hell.

"Yes, no-electricity-no-cars-no-television Amish."

"Yeah, okay, he may be electronically challenged, but is he cute?"

Geoff was so not going there. He lowered his voice, not wanting Len to overhear, because he knew how this was going to sound. "He works for me. It doesn't matter if he's cute, gorgeous, sexy, or a stud and a half. I can't be thinking about him or any of the guys who work for me like that. It wouldn't be right."

"It wouldn't be right for you to *do* anything, but you have eyes. You can look, can't you?"

"Raine! Can we please talk about something else?"

"What else is there to talk about? You moved away to become a poor farmer, leaving the rest of us to fend for ourselves in the big city."

God, Raine could be such a smartass. And Geoff was anything but a poor farmer. He'd reviewed all the accounts and had even gone to the bank to make sure they were right. The farm as it stood did very well, and his dad had set aside ten percent of the profits each year, for God knows how long, in an emergency fund to tide them through lean years. That fund was now enough to run the farm for five years. But there was no way he was telling Raine that. The man would be in the car in five minutes and on the way there to "help" Geoff spend it.

"You could always come for a visit. I'd love to take you riding." Raine on a horse; now that would be a sight.

"Riding what? I only ride one thing, and you know it."

"If you've never been on a horse, then you don't know what you're missing. Fifteen hundred pounds of hot, sweaty, pounding muscle between your legs. What more could you ask?" That set them both cackling to beat the band.

Geoff heard something in the background that sounded like Raine's bell. "I gotta go," Raine said.

"Okay, you have fun. I'll talk to you later." They disconnected and Geoff put the phone back in its cradle and joined Len in the living room.

"Where's Eli?" Geoff asked.

"Probably still in the barn. You know he never comes in until it's almost too dark to see."

"I gotta give him credit, the man works hard, really hard."

Len sat up in his chair. "He does, but I think he also doesn't know what to do with his time. I suspect that his life in the community was quite regimented and full, so when he has extra time, he fills it with more work." Geoff nodded, wondering what Len was getting at. "You go riding every morning—take him with you," Len suggested. "He'd probably enjoy it; you'd have some company, and it would give him something to do besides work."

Geoff swallowed, the conversation with Raine fresh in his mind. But Len was right. It would probably do them both good. "Thanks, Len."

Instead of watching television, Geoff glanced out one of the windows and saw that the lights were still on in the barn. Leaving the room, he walked outside, the dogs greeting him right away. "Come on, pups, let's go see what Eli's doing." He walked toward the barn, the dogs following, their tails wagging.

In the barn, he found Eli by Princess's stall, the young man watching the mother and colt. The dogs ran up to him, and he smiled, patting and scratching the mutts.

"What's up, Eli?"

His attention shifted from the dogs. "Just watching the colt."

"You know you don't have to stay out here. You can come in the house."

Eli shrugged a little. "I know—"

"What is it?" *Shit, of course.* "You're a little homesick, aren't you?" Why hadn't he thought of it before? This was probably the first time in his life that Eli had been away from his family. Of course he was homesick.

"What is homesick?" He looked up at Geoff, those blue eyes huge and longing.

"It means that you miss your family."

"Yes, I'm homesick." Eli looked down, "Not that you haven't been good to me."

"It's only natural that you'd miss your family." Geoff sat down on a hay bale. "The first time I left home, it was to go to summer camp at Stony Lake. I was only going to be away from home for a week, but as soon as my dad left, all I wanted to do was go home. I didn't know any of the other kids, and everything was strange, even the food."

"What happened?"

"After about two hours, I met Matt. After three hours, I was having so much fun swimming and playing with the other kids that I forgot all about being homesick. And before I knew it, the week was over."

"Were you happy when your dad came to get you?"

"Actually, I asked if I could stay another week." The surprised look on Eli's face was priceless. "You see, I'd grown up a little during that week, realized I could get along on my own and have fun doing it."

"What are you saying?"

"I'm saying that maybe you need to add a little fun to your day. Do something you enjoy… for example, riding horses." Eli's face lit up, and Geoff continued, "I go riding almost every morning. It's one of the things I do for fun, and I was wondering if you'd like to join me?"

"Go riding with you?"

"Sure. The horses need exercise, and we need some fun. You don't have to go if you don't want to. I just thought you might enjoy it," Geoff said.

"I would, thank you." The dogs had settled on the floor, crowding around their legs.

"Is there anything else you like to do?" Geoff asked.

"My uncle used to let me help him bake bread, but I don't know how to do that with the oven you have. We use a wood-fired oven."

"It's not that hard. You could make the dough, and I could help you bake it. Dad used to bake bread all the time, so we have the supplies. We could do that tomorrow night if you like."

"That's very nice of you." Eli gave him another of those incredibly bright smiles, and Geoff found himself watching his face—those big, bright eyes, luscious lips, dark hair that threatened to curl. Geoff blinked and stood up a little too fast, startling the dogs. Fuck... fuck... fuck... He was going to kill Raine the next time he saw him.

"Let's go back to the house. It's getting late, and we need to be up early for our ride." Geoff turned and left the barn. As he was crossing the yard, Eli caught up to him, and they entered the house together.

Len was asleep in his chair, and Geoff turned off the television. Len woke almost immediately. "Why don't you go on up to bed?" Geoff said. Len nodded and got out of his chair, and after saying good-night, went up the stairs.

They'd finished moving Len to another bedroom a few days earlier, and they'd finished moving Geoff's things into the master bedroom that afternoon. Geoff heard Len go into his room and shut the door. Eli said good-night and headed upstairs as well, Geoff watching him as he went before chastising himself and turning out the lights. After making sure everything was secure, he went upstairs and walked into his new bedroom. His furniture was in the room, the closet was full of his things, but the bed was the one that had occupied the room for as long as he could remember, as long as anyone could remember.

Standing in the doorway, the house quiet, Geoff stared at the bed, wondering. *Dad and Len had spent their last night together in that bed, knowing that Dad couldn't go on any more, and that this was likely to be their last night together. What did they say to one another? Thank you for twenty years of love—for loving me enough to let me go? Did they just hold one another and say nothing at all?* Geoff would never know, didn't really want to know. *I hope someday I find a love like they had.* With a soft sigh, he went into the room and quietly shut the door.

He'd had reservations about sleeping in that bed, but Len had reassured him. "That bed is lucky. That bed is lucky. Your grand-parents and great-grandparents used it, and your father and I loved in it for twenty years. There's a lot of love that's soaked its way into the wood."

Geoff got undressed, started the shower, and stepped under the hot water. That felt so good, soothing away the day's work, relaxing his muscles, allowing his mind to shut down and wander. His hands roamed and wandered too. It'd been a while, but his body responded to his own hand. Sighing to himself, he tweaked his nipples and slid his hands lower, one cupping his balls, the other stroking, moving slowly along his length. Damn, that felt good. It had been weeks since he'd been with anyone, and his body was tingling, balls full and ready. "Yes…."

He let his mind conjure up pictures of the men he'd always found attractive: big, wide, muscular men with huge pecs and round, bulging arms. The water beat down on him as he slowly, sensuously, worked himself, fingers sliding from base to tip, others lightly pinching his nipples before reaching behind him to tickle his opening. "God…."

He picked up the pace, but nothing really happened. Something wasn't quite right. He just… wasn't… quite… there. Then the vision in his mind changed to a long, lithe body, smooth skin, big blue eyes, black hair. "Fuck…."

His orgasm barreled through him like a runaway train, and he shook as his release shot from him, coating the bathroom tiles.

Geoff leaned against the warm wall, breathing heavily as he recovered from the monster orgasm. Once he could think again, he washed himself thoroughly and cleaned up the tile before turning off the water and drying himself. Then he padded into his bedroom and climbed between the sheets. "Damn you, Raine. I'm going to fucking kill you." But the genie was out of the bottle, and he'd just have to deal with it.

CHAPTER 6

GEOFF loved mornings on the farm: the sun peeking through the windows, the smell of hay and horses, and the quiet before everyone else was up. Throwing back the covers, he looked around and for a second tried to remember where he was, or more importantly, why he was in Len's and his dad's bedroom. *That's right*—it was his room now.

Getting out of bed, he hurried to the bathroom to take care of business and get cleaned up before dressing and walking quietly down the stairs. Len wasn't up yet, and Geoff didn't want to wake him. After grabbing a quick snack, he left the house and strode to the barn. Opening the door, he was very surprised to see Eli already inside, getting the horses brushed and ready for their ride.

"Wow, you didn't have to do that." Geoff got the rugs, handed Eli the one for his horse, and then got the saddles.

"It's okay. I like working with the horses, and he really likes being brushed." Eli tilted his head to indicate Kirk.

Geoff put the saddle on Kirk's back. "That he does; he just loves attention." Geoff fitted Kirk with his bit and bridle and then led him out of his stall and into the yard. "I thought we'd ride down to the creek."

"I'll follow you then." Eli mounted and walked his horse into the pasture with Geoff following a few seconds later,

Kirk was jumpy, raring to go. "Meet you on the far side!" Geoff spurred Kirk on, and the horse took off, running like the wind across the field. Kirk flew under him, and he could feel his spirit meld with the horse, the two of them working together. As he approached the far end of the field, he reined Kirk in and turned to wait for Eli, who came galloping up a minute later, and Geoff got to watch as he and Twilight glided across the field. Wow, the man looked good in a saddle… hot, even.

Before he could chastise himself for the thought, Eli approached, reining in Twilight. Grinning to beat the band, he puffed, "That felt so good."

"Didn't it? And the best part is that we get to do it again on the way back." Geoff found himself grinning. Eli's excitement was contagious. "We'll walk them to the creek and then head east for a while." Geoff led the way along the trail, both of them quiet, getting a little lost in their thoughts under a canopy of green and a carpet of spring wildflowers. At the creek, they stopped for a few minutes, listening to the water, and then turned where the trail followed the creek. "In the summer when I was a kid, I used to play in the creek all the time."

"Wasn't it cold?"

"You bet it was, but I was a kid. I'd play in the water for hours until my teeth rattled." Geoff smiled at the memory. "I used to ride back here with my dad and Len when it was hot, and we'd have a picnic in the clearing up ahead. I'd play in the water, and they'd talk." Those were some of his fondest childhood memories. "What I wouldn't give to be able to go riding just one more time with him."

"When did he die?"

"About a month ago. He'd had cancer for a while. He was only forty-nine." Geoff choked down the emotions that threatened to bubble to the surface. He looked at Eli and could almost see the questions spinning through the young man's head.

"I'm sorry about your dad. What happened to your mother?"

"She died when I was still a baby. I don't have any memory of her, just the few pictures that are hanging on the wall in the living room."

They reached the clearing, and Geoff dismounted. Kirk started to wander around, munching on the fresh grass. "We can sit here if you want." Eli dismounted and looked around, holding the reins. "They won't go anywhere; they like it here." Eli looked skeptical but flipped the reins over the saddle, and Twilight started to munch on the grass just like Kirk, happy as anything.

Geoff sat on a fallen log, watching and listening to the water as Eli sat next to him. "I don't want to pry, but can I ask you a question?" Eli asked. Geoff nodded slowly.

"Is Len your uncle?"

This was the question Geoff had been dreading for some time. He'd already determined that he was going to tell Eli the truth, but he wasn't sure how to make him understand. He'd done some Internet research, so he knew what the Amish taught about homosexuality, and if he was being frank with himself, he was concerned that the answer would drive Eli away. "No, Len was my dad's partner."

Eli started to say something, but Geoff stopped him. "There's something you have to understand, and I'm going to ask you to keep

63

an open mind." Eli nodded. "Len and my father were lovers. They loved each other, took care of each other, and raised me together for almost my whole life."

Eli's mouth gaped open. "You mean Len and your dad were sodomites?"

"We use the term 'gay', but yes." Geoff watched as Eli swallowed hard, saying nothing, his expression unreadable. "I know what the Bible says about it, but there's something else you need to know. Len and my dad loved each other deeply for more than twenty years. They helped each other, took care of each other when they were sick, took care of me—I just don't see how that kind of love can be wrong."

"I've heard about people like them, but I never met anyone like that before. Len seems so nice, I...." Eli's words trailed off, and Geoff could see the confusion on his face.

"Eli, I know this is hard for you to reconcile with what you've been taught all your life, but think about this for me." Those incredible blue eyes rose from the ground, boring into Geoff's with the intensity of a hurricane. "The Bible says a lot about many things, but the one thing it always says is good is love. Dad and Len loved each other very much, and the rest just doesn't matter." Geoff stood up and paced around the clearing before stopping to pat Kirk's neck, waiting for whatever Eli had to say.

"Does that make you... like them?"

"Eli, the proper word is 'gay', and yes, I'm gay, but not because of them. It wasn't something they taught me. It's just the way I am, just like I have brown hair and brown eyes. It's part of the way I was made." Eli sat there, his face stony. "I'm sorry if this makes you uncomfortable, and if you want to leave, I'll make arrangements for your pay as soon as we get back to the farm. I won't hold it against you. It's a lot for you to accept." Geoff could see the turmoil continue behind Eli's eyes, and he waited for whatever he decided.

"You and Len have been good to me, both of you. And one of the reasons that I'm taking a year away from the community is because I've been having troubles with some of the teachings. Papa says I'm rebellious and that I don't think right about things."

"What are you saying?"

"You've been truthful with me, so I need to be truthful with you."

Geoff sat back down as Eli continued.

"Papa stays very close to the old ways. Others in the community have telephones or will ride in cars, but not Papa. Not even for business, which even the elders say is acceptable." Eli hung his head like he was ashamed of something.

"Eli, you have nothing to be ashamed of. One of the things about being gay is that you tend to accept people for who they are. I won't judge you, I promise."

"I have always looked at things differently from Papa. He says that telephones are wrong and that we should never use them, so he conducts all his business in person. I argued with him that they were allowed for business and that he would be able to get more work if he used one. He didn't have to have one in the house; he could use the community telephone, but he yelled at me and told me not to talk back to him. When I didn't turn away, he hit me on the side of my head and told me to never mention it again."

"He hit you?"

"Not hard. Just to emphasize that I should not to argue with him. The point is that I tend to think too much, and I don't think the way most in the community think. That's why my Papa and uncle, the one with the bakery, thought I should spend a year away. They

65

want me to find out how hard life is outside the community so I'll come back, marry, have children, and take over for Papa."

"What about your mother? What does she think?"

"I don't know. Papa runs the family, and mother goes along with whatever he says. She wouldn't dare oppose him. She'd be brought before the church and shamed in front of everyone."

Geoff didn't like the sound of that. "'Shamed', what's that?"

"When you break one of the community's laws, you are brought before the entire community in church, and the minister tells everyone what you did. If you do it again, they might kick you out."

"Kick you out of what?" Geoff was finding it a little hard to follow.

"The community will shun you—pretend you don't exist. Completely ignore you. I saw it happen once about five years ago. One man's wife accused him of not having proper marital relations."

Geoff wasn't sure what he meant, but he decided not to interrupt.

Eli explained. "He was found in his barn by his wife, taking himself in hand."

"That's against the rules?" Good God, he was glad he wasn't Amish; he'd done that so many times as a teenager, he'd have been shunned for sure.

Eli nodded. "At first they shamed him in church, telling everyone what he'd done, but he did it again. This time, the whole community shunned him. They wouldn't have anything to do with him, his wife, or his children. Eventually they left the community, I guess, because I never saw any of them again. There were rumors about one man in the community, that he was...." Geoff could almost see Eli choosing his words. "Like Len. Some people shunned him just based on the rumor."

"It sounds harsh." Actually, it sounded beyond harsh to Geoff. To those who fit in, it was probably easy, but to those who didn't fit the mold, it could be very difficult.

"I don't want you to think we're all harsh. We have fun, too, and my family loves me. That's why they gave me the year away, so I could come back and fit better in the community."

Geoff looked at his watch. They'd been talking for a while, and they had things to do. "We should be getting back." He stood up and took Kirk's reins, mounting the horse with ease, and waited for Eli to do the same with Twilight. "Whatever you decide, I'll respect your decision."

Eli and Twilight walked up next to him. "I'd like to stay if I can. You and Len have been nice to me, and part of the purpose of a year away is to spend time with people who are different."

"I'm glad." Geoff really was. He had worried about how he was going to tell Eli, but the young man seemed to accept the news well and was willing to stay.

"Yesterday you said that you'd show me how to use the oven thing so I could make bread. Can we do that today?" Eli's eyes were wide with hope and expectation.

"Sure. Once our chores are done."

They headed down the trail and back toward the pasture. The sun was bright and warming as they emerged from the woods. At the edge of the pasture, Geoff watched as Eli gave Twilight her head and the two of them raced across the field. Kirk was itching to follow, and when Geoff gave him the signal, he was off.

When they reached the barn, they unsaddled their mounts and brushed them again before making sure each had plenty of water and oats. They then went back to the house where Len had breakfast waiting. Eli ate quickly and took off for the barn to get his chores done.

Len cleared the plate. "Looks like you two had a good ride this morning. He's so happy he could barely sit still."

"He asked if I'd show him how to use the oven so he could bake bread. I think he's feeling a little homesick. And yes, the ride was exhilarating. We rode to the clearing where you and dad used to take me as a kid for picnics."

"I haven't been there in some time."

"He asked if you were my uncle."

"What did you tell him?"

"The truth. I was concerned how he'd react, but I'm not ashamed of you or my dad." Geoff smiled. "It seems that our Eli has a bit of a rebellious streak in him. He took the news remarkably well and told me some things about himself."

"You like him, don't you."

"Yes, he's a nice kid and a good worker."

"Don't you try to fool me. I've seen the way you look at him and the way he looks at you." Geoff snapped his head around so fast his neck hurt, but Len just smiled. "You can't tell me that lovely young man with that angelic face hasn't caught your eye, and I know he's been watching you."

"Look, Len...." The confrontational tone Geoff was about to use slipped away. "He's one of the men; he works for me. I can't think about him that way, and you know it. And as for him looking at me, I think you're seeing things."

"Maybe, but I know you. Just be careful." Len got up from the table. A firm hand clasped Geoff's shoulder, and then Len went outside, calling to the men, getting them started.

Geoff cleaned up the kitchen and went to the office, spending the day with the books, still working on getting them up to date. At lunchtime, Len brought him a sandwich, and he ate and kept at it, determined to get this done. It had taken him a few weeks, but by the end of the day, he had everything together and computerized so he could spend more time working and less time with the books.

As he was finishing up, he heard the back door open, and Eli called his name.

"I'm in the office."

Eli came in holding his hat. "I was wondering if now was a good time?" Eli would work himself to the bone, but every time he asked for anything, he was almost apologetic.

Geoff knew this was part of his upbringing, but it made him a little angry every time he saw it. He kept that to himself—saying anything to Eli would only upset him and would probably be interpreted as an attack on the community. "It's the perfect time. My eyes are crossing, I've spent so much time in here." He closed the books, shut off the computer, and turned out the light. "Let's go bake some bread."

Geoff led the way to the kitchen, opening cupboards and pulling out bowls, spoons, and measuring cups. "I know some of these things are different from what you're used to. I hope you can manage."

"I should be able to." Eli watched as Geoff got out some whole wheat flour. At least this Eli would be used to. Dad had gotten it at the Amish bakery.

"What else do you need?"

"Yeast, salt, milk, a little sugar, and some water." Geoff got the ingredients together while Eli started setting everything the way he wanted it. "I need a board." Geoff got one from one of the cabinets. Then Eli went to work measuring the ingredients. He looked up, smiling, "Do you want to help?" Geoff smiled back and stood next to Eli. "You can measure the flour." Eli told him how much, and Geoff started measuring it out, pouring it into the bowl.

Just as he was finishing, the bag slipped and a handful of flour hit the counter and sprayed back up in a white cloud, covering them both. To Geoff's relief, Eli started to laugh, and he joined in, the two of them shaking their clothes and sending more flour dust into the air, covering them both in white.

"You look like a ghost," Eli teased.

"And you look like a demented snowman." The laughter was infectious, and every time one of them would stop, the other would start again, flour going everywhere. At one point, Len walked in, took one look around, and walked right back out again, shaking his head and not saying a word.

Finally, the laughter subsided, and the air cleared. Eli's eyes were dancing with delight, and Geoff felt his breath catch a little but refrained from turning away. That face was just too happy not to look at. "I need to get this flour out of my shirt." It was starting to itch. Geoff unbuttoned and took off his shirt and opened the back door, shaking out the flour. He came back inside and put his shirt back on, watching Eli as he did. Maybe Len was right; Eli did seem to be watching him pretty closely. Once he had his shirt on, he went back to work and finished measuring out the flour, watching Eli out of the corner of his eye as the young man took off his own shirt and waved it outside to shake off the flour. Geoff didn't get more than a few seconds' peek at his skin, but what he saw was flawless. *Damn....*

Geoff kept his mind on the task at hand as they finished the bread dough and set it to rise. They spent the next half hour cleaning up the flour, but it took Geoff a lot longer than that to get the image of Eli's bare chest and bright smile out of his mind.

CHAPTER 7

"JESUS CHRIST, I'm glad that's done." Geoff walked stiffly into the kitchen, hanging his hat on the rack near the door. "I swear I planted half of Mason County in the last week." His legs hurt and his rear hurt, but he kept moving, trying to keep his muscles from seizing up.

Len got up from the table and brought him a cup of coffee, "You did really good. After the rain last week, I didn't think we'd get everything planted in time. But you did."

Geoff started to sit but thought better of it. "I feel like I have that tractor seat attached to my butt, but I got it done." He actually felt really good, like he'd accomplished something pretty amazing. All the fields were planted, and it was still a week before Memorial Day. Granted, it had almost killed him, but it was done.

"Did Eli like driving the tractor?" Len asked. Geoff gave him a "how did you know?" look. "I saw the two of you when I was going into town this afternoon."

"Yeah, he seemed to. At first he was nervous, but then he really seemed to get into it. I think he likes trying new things." Eli really was an Amish rebel.

"You should go to bed." Geoff nodded and went upstairs, passing Eli as he made his way to his room.

"Geoff, are you all right?" The concern in Eli's voice made him stop and turn.

Geoff smiled; the tightness in the face he'd come to think of as almost angelic was really touching. "I'm fine, just really tired."

"You can barely walk." Eli stepped toward him, taking his arm and helping him into the bedroom, settling him on the side of the bed. "Are you sure you're all right?"

"Yes, just *really* tired." The concerned look on Eli's face made Geoff want to reach out and kiss a smile into its place. In fact, he found himself leaning forward slightly, but he pulled back. He couldn't, he just couldn't take the chance. He'd spent the last two weeks trying not to think of Eli as anything other than another of the farm hands, but it was becoming more and more difficult. Besides, he didn't really know if Eli was even interested, and even if he was…. He had to stop thinking this way. Eli was just another of the farm hands and had to be treated just like the other men. "Thanks for helping me. I'll be fine."

Eli turned to leave the room. "I'll see you in the morning." Then he was gone, and Geoff slowly got his tired, aching muscles to work. Getting undressed, he managed to get himself into the bathroom and under the spray of a hot shower. The water felt good on his body but did nothing to calm his mind or drive away the thoughts he kept having about Eli. He knew he had to get himself under control, or he'd do something he'd regret. "This is something I just have to keep to myself and can't act on, no matter what."

Geoff knew he was developing feelings for the angelic, innocent young Amish man, feelings he shouldn't be having and most definitely couldn't act on.

With a sigh, he turned off the water and stepped out of the shower, drying himself off. He took some ibuprofen against the pain he knew was to come and climbed into bed, falling asleep almost as soon as his head hit the pillow.

He woke at the usual time, his body protesting each and every movement. He hadn't felt this bad since the last time he'd been out drinking all night, and at least then he'd had sex. Forcing his legs to move, he got to the bathroom and took some more pain relievers. Somehow he got himself dressed and presentable before dragging himself down to the kitchen, where a pot of coffee was blessedly waiting. Pouring himself a mug, he sipped as he walked slowly around the kitchen, loosening up tightened muscles.

Once he'd finished his coffee, he put his mug in the sink and walked carefully to the barn to see what was going on. He had no intention of going riding—the thought of trying to get on a horse made his legs throb. Opening the door, he saw movement in one of the stalls and figured it was Eli with Twilight. Sure enough, he found Eli in Twilight's stall, tightening the girth on her saddle. "Morning, Eli."

The smile he got lit the entire barn. "Good morning, Geoff. Feeling better?"

"Yes, and thank you for helping me."

Eli smiled, nodded, and went back to saddling Twilight. Geoff went down to Kirk's stall, and that majestic black head poked out as soon as he heard footsteps. "Morning, boy." He patted his nose and was about to give him a carrot when he noticed the bit and bridle. Looking in the stall he saw that Kirk had been brushed and groomed until his coat gleamed, with his saddle on his back. Every morning for the last week, Geoff had come out to find Kirk saddled and ready for their morning ride.

"Okay, boy, I guess we're going after all." He heard Eli leading Twilight out of the barn, so he opened the stall door and led Kirk out too. "Eli, thank you, but you don't have to saddle him for me." Eli's smile faded, and Geoff knew he had to say something, anything to get that smile back. "He looks beautiful." Geoff smiled, and Eli's returned full force.

They mounted their horses, Geoff far more gingerly than usual, and headed out. The sun had just risen, and the cool May morning was refreshing and crisp. They talked very little, just riding together, passing fields of wildflowers and pastures with grazing cattle.

Eli rode up next to him. "Geoff, I'm not sure how to ask this, but here in the English world, is it okay to be...." He stopped, and Geoff waited for him to continue. "You know... gay?"

They hadn't spoken on this topic since their morning ride a few weeks earlier, and Geoff had figured it was because Eli wasn't comfortable talking about it.

"I've been thinking since we talked, and I wanted to ask," Eli continued. "In the community, if someone was gay, they'd be excommunicated... are the English the same way?"

"That's a difficult question. For a long time, people could be killed or put in prison for being gay, but now most people are more understanding. There are still people who won't accept us and even those who would hurt us. But most people are understanding, and quite frankly, most people really don't care anymore. As an example, Lumpy, Pete, and Fred all knew about Len and my dad. It didn't matter to them, but my Aunt Janelle still can't accept it even after all these years."

"Oh." Eli seemed more confused now than he was before he asked the question.

"Let me ask you something. My being gay doesn't bother you, does it?" Eli shook his head. "Why not?"

Eli thought for a minute. "Because you're a kind person who's been good to me. And I guess I feel you're right; it shouldn't matter who you love."

"Then you answered your own question. What's important is being a good person, caring for others, and treating other people the way you want to be treated: with respect and dignity. If you do that, good people will see you for who you are and the rest can go to hell." Geoff gestured and laughed a little. "Does that help you?"

Now it was Eli's turn to smile. "Yeah." They rode the rest of the way in near silence, returning to the barn an hour after they left. Geoff felt much better. The ride had gotten him some fresh air, and his muscles felt warm and loose. They finished unsaddling their horses and headed in for breakfast.

The kitchen smelled heavenly with breakfast cooking. On his way to the sink, Geoff leaned against the table to smell the bouquet of wildflowers on the table. Len always gathered them each spring, and it made him happy that Len was carrying on with his life. With a final glance at the flowers, he went to wash his hands. "Is that fresh cinnamon raisin bread I smell?"

Len didn't look up from his eggs. "Yup."

"Thank you for making it." His dad had made bread, but Len made cinnamon raisin bread that was to die for. Len brought him his plate and set it in front of him. "Thank you."

"You're welcome, but I didn't make the bread. Eli did." Geoff took a bite of the toast and moaned softly. The butter and cinnamon melted together, sliding down his throat. That was heavenly.

The door opened, and Eli took his place at the table, with Len putting his plate in front of him.

"Thank you for the bread, it's delicious," Geoff said. He got the same smile he'd seen when he brought out Kirk that morning, all happy and pleased.

"I'm glad it turned out. I'd never made it before." Eli started eating, and Len joined them at the table with his own plate. The conversation turned to the activities for the day.

"I've got to get the books done; tomorrow's payday," Geoff said.

Len swallowed. "The rest of us will be repairing fences this morning and checking on the herds this afternoon. Lumpy thinks he might have seen the signs of wolves, so we need to check it out."

"I'll have lunch ready for you." Geoff took his plate to the sink and went into the office to get started. He heard the others leave and breathed a sigh of relief before picking up the phone and calling Raine.

"This had better be good, calling me at this godawful hour."

Geoff looked at the clock; it was after eight. "I've been up for hours. Shit, I forgot it's an hour earlier there. Sorry, Raine."

He heard a yawn on the other end of the line. "What's so important that it couldn't wait until a decent hour?"

"Raine, I don't know what to do. I've tried everything, but I just can't stop thinking about him."

"What? Who? Geoff, who are you talking about?"

"Eli." God, this was such a mistake.

"Wait...." Geoff could almost hear the smile on Raine's face. "You're calling me because you like this Eli and he doesn't like you?"

"No, he doesn't know how I feel about him. Eli's the Amish guy who works for me."

"Holy crap! You're telling me you're in love with an Amish guy? Look, my mind's not working too well yet. It's early. Why don't you spell it out for me so I can try to help you?"

Geoff took a deep breath. "I told you about Eli already."

"Wait a minute. You're calling me all flustered at some early hour about Eli. Let me guess; you really like him?"

"Yes, but I shouldn't like him that way."

"Why not? Does he know you're gay?"

"Yes, we talked about it, and I told him."

"Does he like you?"

"I don't know. Raine, I don't even know if he's gay. That's the first problem." Raine tried to interrupt on the other side of the line, but Geoff cut him off. "He's on his year away from the Amish community. What if he's only curious and I hurt him, or worse, we do something and they find out, shun him, and ruin his life?" A host of awful possibilities passed through his mind.

"And what if he loves you back?"

That stopped Geoff in his tracks.

Raine continued. "You wouldn't be so concerned about him if you didn't care for him. But what if he cares for you? I know you believe in true love. You saw it with your dad and Len. What if he's your true love?"

"I... don't know what it's like to be in love... not like that. All I've ever had are meaningless affairs and one-night stands."

"Then maybe it's time you found out. I'm not saying you should rush into anything, but I think you need to look at your feelings honestly and then try to determine his."

"But he's so innocent and sweet and beautiful. What if I ruin that?"

"You won't. I know you. You'll cherish it and make it grow like those horses of yours you love so much." Geoff heard Raine shuffling through his apartment. "Look, babe, I gotta get ready for work. I know this is going to sound cliché, but follow your heart. Look, I gotta go or I'll be late. Call me later and let me know what happens. Bye, babe." The line disconnected. and Geoff hung up the phone.

He sat behind his desk and let his mind wander a little. If he were honest with himself, he really did like Eli... a lot. The way he looked in the saddle, the way he smiled, the way those eyes danced when he was happy. "Fuck, I've got it bad. Now if I just knew how he felt." Geoff had always had good gaydar, but where Eli was concerned, he didn't have a clue.

Finally, he was able to pull his attention back to business, and he got to work, updating the ledgers and writing the paychecks for the men. By the time he was done, it was time to start lunch.

In the kitchen, he made a number of sandwiches and brewed fresh coffee. No sooner was he done than the door opened and the men came in. On days like this when they were fixing fences, it was easier for them to eat at the farm, so Geoff made sure there was plenty. The conversation swirled around work; what they'd accomplished, and what they had to do that afternoon.

"The fences in the far west pasture are falling down. We have to repair them before we can move any cattle in there," Len said.

"Is that what we're doing this afternoon?"

Len looked at Geoff. "We? I thought you had work to do here."

"I got it finished, so I thought I'd help."

All the men smiled and nodded. The more help, the quicker they'd finish.

Once lunch was over, Geoff piled the dishes in the sink, met the guys in the yard, and rode with the rest of the crew to the pasture, where they broke up into teams to dig post holes, set the posts, and finally string the fence. Geoff and Eli worked together to set the posts, making sure they were perfectly vertical before filling the holes. After hours of working, they had the pasture fences repaired and solid. When Len saw the job was finished, everyone piled in the truck for the ride back to the farmhouse. After putting their tools away, Len declared the day's work over, and everyone went inside for dinner and the weekly poker game.

Everyone, that is, except Eli, who went to the barn. Geoff followed to see if something was wrong. "Eli, would you like to join the card game?"

He shook his head. "I can't. You're playing poker, gambling."

Geoff nodded. "I see. Well, you can still join us for dinner, and then the evening is yours to do whatever you'd like. Or you can watch if you want. Whatever you do, I don't want you to work, okay?" Eli nodded, and Geoff led him back toward the house.

They had a nice dinner with everyone chipping in to get it ready, and then they sat around the table, playing cards and talking. Eli sat next to Geoff, watching him through the hands. At the end of the night, everyone helped clean up and then headed home. Eli said good-night and went up to bed. Geoff was left in the kitchen with Len.

"Geoff, you've seemed out of sorts for a while. Is everything okay?" Len sat at the table across from Geoff, a concerned look on his face.

"Yeah, I'm just trying to work through something."

Geoff's sigh was met by a knowing smile. "That something wouldn't have anything to do with Eli, would it?"

Geoff nodded slowly. "I can't stop thinking about him, and I think I'm developing feelings for him, but I—"

"You're not sure if he likes you the same way?"

"Yeah."

Len started snickering and then laughed outright, covering his mouth with his hand to keep himself from getting too loud. "Good God, boy, what do you want him to do, hire a skywriter?"

Len was shaking his head and kept chuckling, which only deepened Geoff's confusion. What had he missed?

"Let me see, each morning for the last week or so, your horse is groomed till he shines and saddled ready for you ride with him."

"Yeah, so?" Geoff shrugged, and Len shook his head again.

"Each morning, when you come down for breakfast, there are fresh flowers on the table."

"I thought you picked those, like you always did for dad."

Len shook his head. "I haven't been picking those. Eli has. And yesterday, he asked me what your favorite bread was, looked up a recipe, and made it for you. Grinned like a cat when you said how much you liked it."

"What is it you're driving at?"

Len shook his head again and rolled his eyes at the ceiling, "He's courting you, ya dummy."

Geoff almost fell out of his chair. There was no way….

Oh my God.

Oh my freaking God. Geoff shook his head slowly as Len smiled and kept nodding.

"In Amish culture, when you like someone, you groom your horses so they look their best, polish your tack until it shines, and take the object of your affection for a buggy ride. He doesn't have a buggy, so he's been saddling your horse and polishing your saddle for the last week, bringing you flowers, making you what you like to eat." Len got up from the table. "Tomorrow, I suggest that you let the boy know his efforts have been noticed and that you're interested. 'Cause if you're not, he can bloody well court me." With those final words, Len went upstairs, still shaking his head.

CHAPTER 8

GEOFF was up early on Saturday. Hell, the sun wasn't even up, and he was out of bed, dressed, and in the barn. "Yes," he whispered as he walked into the dark barn. "I beat you this morning."

Large heads poked out of their stalls, and Geoff stroked and patted each nose as he headed to the tack room to get the supplies. The horses were losing their winter coats, so Geoff grabbed a curry comb, brush, and treats, and then headed to Twilight's stall.

"Hey, girl." He stroked his hand across her side and saw that inquisitive head turn to look at him. "I know; I'm not Eli, but I'll have to do." He gave her a carrot and led her to the grooming area and began brushing her out. She really liked it and moved slightly into his touch. "Feels good, girl. Yeah, I know it does." He was just talking to keep her calm and to fill the dark morning with some reassuring sound. Once she was combed, he brushed her out, making her coat look its best. Then he got her blanket and saddle, placing them on her back and tightening the girth, and led her back to her stall. He'd put her bridle on when they were ready to leave.

Once Twilight was finished, he went to Kirk's stall and got him combed, brushed, and saddled. Just as he was finishing, he heard the barn door open and a soft whistling as Eli entered.

He heard Eli stop a minute to talk to Twilight. "Morning, girl." Then Eli moved on down to Kirk's stall.

"Oh, you're here." Eli looked disappointed and backed out of the stall, walking back to Twilight. Geoff heard a sharp intake of breath and then a soft sigh. He finished saddling Kirk and led him out of the stall, meeting Eli and Twilight on the grass. "Thank you," Eli said. His eyes gleamed, and Geoff smiled back, realizing that the initial message he'd wanted to send had been received.

"You're welcome, and thank you for the flowers and the cinnamon bread." That earned Geoff a grin and a happy sparkle in those blue eyes.

Eli mounted the horse, settling himself into the saddle. "Where are we riding today?"

"Why don't you choose?" Geoff mounted as well and waited for Eli to lead the way out of the yard, and to his surprise, onto the shoulder of the road.

"There's a river up north of us about a half mile. There should be some wonderful wildflowers this time of year." Geoff smiled and followed Eli's lead. At the corner near the farm, they turned north, the horses walking alongside the road, their hooves occasionally clopping on the pavement. There weren't many cars, and those there were passed them carefully.

As they approached the river, a car passed them, moving fast, honking the horn as it sped by. The sound startled Kirk, and he reared, and Geoff went flying. He'd fallen off horses before and rolled as he hit the ground, but he was too close to the edge of the road and began rolling down the ravine toward the river.

"Geoff!" He heard Eli cry in fear.

Finally he stopped himself from rolling, just before he hit the water.

"Geoff." There was a touch of panic in Eli's voice. "Are you okay?"

Geoff was having trouble breathing and couldn't answer; the wind had been knocked out of him when he hit his back. Slowly, he began to breathe again, his lungs beginning to fill and function. "Eli, I'm okay." *I think.* "Don't try to climb down." He heard a car stop and someone talking to Eli. Taking stock, Geoff found he could move his arms and legs. His neck and back didn't hurt. Yeah, he was okay. Slowly, he started getting to his feet. "Is Kirk okay?"

"Yes." There was a definite note of worry in Eli's voice. "A lady stopped to help."

"Good. I'm going to climb up." Geoff slowly got to his feet and began climbing the ravine. He was covered in mud, but everything seemed to be working. It definitely could have been worse. Reaching the top, he saw Eli holding Twilight and, of all people, his Aunt Vicki holding Kirk—and the horse was not happy, shaking his head, his eyes rolling.

"Thank you for stopping." Geoff took Kirk from her, patting his neck and soothing the agitated horse.

"Are you okay? I saw what happened. Didn't even slow down, the bastard!" The indignation was plain in her voice, enough for both of them.

"Yeah, I'm okay. Nothing hurts but my pride." Cars were passing occasionally, and each one spooked Kirk a little bit more. "We should get back. Why don't you meet us at the farm for breakfast?"

His aunt nodded and headed to her car. "I'll meet you at the house." She got into her car, turned it around, and sped off.

Geoff started walking back. "There's a trail through the woods that leads to the farm just ahead. We can mount again once we're away from the road."

"I'm sorry." Eli sighed softly behind him.

Geoff stopped and turned around, seeing the pained look on Eli's face. "There's nothing to be sorry for. It was the driver's fault, not yours. He's the one who behaved badly, so don't feel bad." He wanted to soothe away the hurt he saw on Eli's face.

"But I'm the one who suggested we come this way."

"Eli, you're not responsible for the behavior of others—only yourself, and you did nothing wrong." He waited for Eli to catch up. "I mean it. I'm okay, and I really appreciate your concern." Before he could stop himself, he reached out and stroked his hand along Eli's cheek. "Thank you."

They reached the trail and walked the horses away from the road. Kirk had calmed down, and Geoff was able to mount him, and they slowly walked back, the feel of Eli's skin against his palm still fresh in his mind.

Once they reached the farm, unsaddled the horses, and turned them out into the pastures for the day, Geoff spoke. "Tomorrow is your day off, and I thought instead of riding first thing in the morning, we could ride after breakfast, someplace extra fun."

As they walked toward the house, Eli agreed timidly. "Okay."

"Then I'll meet you in the yard at nine; I'll take care of everything." Geoff was smiling to beat the band. He'd just had a great idea... one he was sure Eli would like.

In the kitchen, Geoff found his Aunt Vicki sitting at the table, drinking coffee.

"I really wanted to talk to you," she said. Geoff poured himself a cup and sat down across from her. "Janelle told me about the incident in the store. She made it sound as though you'd accosted her." Geoff began to say something, but she quieted him. "I know you did no such thing, and I want to know what really happened."

Geoff sighed. "She said some awful things about Len and Dad and then accused me of corrupting Joey and Eli. Dad put up with her for all those years. Why, I have no idea, but I do know she's got a problem with me being gay."

Aunt Vicki sighed. "There's some history there that you don't know—and don't need to know—but your Aunt Janelle is a bitter and unhappy person. For the longest time I took her side, but this has got to stop." She sipped her coffee and then set down her cup. "I wanted you to know that I don't feel the same way she does, and I told her she needs to let it go." She stood up to go.

Geoff was shocked as shit. Vicki and Janelle had been as thick as thieves for as long as he could remember. He stood up and gave her a hug. "Thank you."

"She's my sister, and I love her, but sometimes the woman can be a right pain in the ass." She returned his hug. "And I want you to know that the quilt is just a symbol. You do with it what you think best." She left as Len came in and started making breakfast, the two of them exchanging greetings as they passed.

"What did she want?" Len mused as he started breakfast.

"To let me know that she's not Aunt Janelle." Geoff watched as she got into her car and drove away.

While they were eating breakfast, the guys showed up, and Geoff gave them their paychecks. Payday was usually on Monday, but Geoff had told the men that he would have everything ready on Saturday if they wanted to stop by. Len poured cups of coffee, and everyone chatted. Even though it was Saturday, there were still

87

chores to be done and animals to feed, but the workload was much less than during the week, so the chores were divvied up and everyone left, getting done quickly so they could have the rest of the day free. Joey walked in as the guys were leaving, so he and Len went out for his lesson.

The rest of the day was typical for a Saturday. In the afternoon it rained, so they spent the time relaxing and watching a few movies, with Geoff checking the Weather Channel from time to time.

In the morning, Geoff got up and brushed the horses before pulling the truck and trailer around to the barn door. He loaded the blankets, saddles, and tack into the bins inside and then loaded the horses. To his surprise, both Kirk and Twilight went in without a fuss. Maybe they were getting used to him, or maybe it was the treats he'd placed in the feed bags. He closed the door of the horse trailer.

"Morning, Geoff." Eli was looking at the truck and trailer very curiously. "What's this?"

"It's a horse trailer." Geoff checked that everything was secure, went inside to get the cooler and lunch he'd packer earlier, and met Eli by the truck. "Get in. We're going for a ride." Eli looked a little dubious, but opened the door and got into the truck. Geoff started the engine and slowly pulled down the drive and onto the road. He drove carefully, taking the country roads until he got close to town, and then he turned onto Ludington Avenue as they headed toward the lake. Eli was watching everything, taking it all in as they drove.

"Have you been here before?" Geoff asked.

He nodded his head slowly. "Papa only went into Scottville, and only when he absolutely had to, but my uncle sells bread on the road to the state park during the summer, so I've been here with him a few times." They turned north onto Lakeshore Drive. "Are we going to the state park?"

"Yes, I thought we could ride on the beach."

Eli's face lit like a beacon. "I've never been any closer than the cutoff where Uncle sells bread."

"Then you're in for a treat. I thought we could park the trailer, unload the horses, and ride up the beach to the lighthouse, have a picnic, and then ride back."

Eli was so excited, he was practically bouncing, and Geoff smiled at the younger man's excitement. They drove for a good ten or fifteen minutes before reaching the park entrance. Geoff waved to the ranger as they passed through the gate and then pulled into the first parking lot. "The lake is just over there." He pointed, and Eli got out, running in that direction. Geoff shook his head as he got out of the truck and began unloading the horses.

Eli returned, excitement written all over his face. "The lake's so big you can't see the other side." He loved Eli's innocence, the look on his face when he saw something new, but it scared him too.

"There's a pan in the back of the truck. Would you fill it from the jugs? I want the horses to have a drink before we start." Eli rushed off and got the pan, filling it with water. Eli held Twilight's reins while she drank, and Geoff unloaded Kirk and let him drink as well.

"You'll need a jacket; there's one for you in the back seat," Geoff said.

When they were ready, they put away the pan, shut and locked the truck, and walked the horses across the parking lot and onto the beach.

The breeze was brisk and refreshing as they rode north down the beach. The sound of the waves and wind, gulls and boats, the smell of the water and the horses, the sun on the waves and the swath of sand all combined to fill their senses. They rode side by side, watching each other as the horses walked along.

"This is so beautiful. I never knew...." The rest of what Eli said was carried away by the wind, but Geoff could see the delight on Eli's face, and he returned his smile.

Beneath him, Geoff could feel Kirk straining, wanting to run, but it was too dangerous. The sand held many things that couldn't be seen until it was too late, so he kept talking to him, keeping him calm. Slowly, he could feel the tension leave his mount, just like his own worries and cares blew away with the wind.

Eli pointed as something tall appeared on the horizon. Geoff signaled to the horses, and they both stopped. "That's the Point Sable Lighthouse."

"But what is it?"

"Ships use them to determine where they are at night. That one was built in the 1860s. We can go right up to it, and you can climb it if you want."

"Yeah?"

"Sure, come on." They rode the rest of the way and dismounted as they approached the break wall. Eli looked up at the lighthouse. "There are stairs on the inside. I'll stay here with the horses." Eli nodded and started walking toward the door. Geoff watched, and ten minutes later, he saw Eli waving at him from the railing. He waved back and watched as he circled the light, looking out in every direction. He waved again and then disappeared, reappearing at ground level, running toward him.

"That was...." Eli tried to describe the feeling but couldn't. "That was unbelievable. I never knew you could go so high, and the wind, it felt like it wanted me to fly."

"I know. There's a great view of the beach and the park from up there." There were surprisingly few people around, "We can tie the horses to that post and sit for a while."

Eli smiled, and they tethered the horses, sitting at a picnic table nearby.

"There's something that I want to talk to you about, and you may find it difficult. But I don't want there to be any misunderstanding." Eli's eyes widened, but he met Geoff's gaze, curious about what Geoff wanted to know. "This is hard for me too."

"Then just speak plain."

Geoff smiled to himself—spoken like an Amish man. "I think I know why you've been grooming and saddling my horse each morning, bringing in wildflowers, and baking my favorite bread. And I have to ask you plain, are you courting me?"

Eli's smile faded and color rose in his cheeks as his gaze shifted down to the table top. *Shit... I was wrong and I've embarrassed him.*

"I'm sorry if I did something wrong." Eli got up from the table and walked toward the lake, turning his back to Geoff, shoulders slumped.

"Eli... Eli," Geoff got up and touched the young man's shoulder. "Eli...."

He turned around, eyes full, the tears ready to spill down his wind reddened cheeks.

"Eli, you didn't do anything wrong. I was just asking because I needed to be sure. After all, by bringing you here today, I was sort of courting you."

"You were?" Eli wiped his eyes.

"Come sit down." Eli followed Geoff back to the table and sat, wiping the moisture from his eyes. "I just wanted to be sure. Because there are other questions I need you to think about." Eli nodded. "You have to know that what you're doing will not be condoned by your family or others in the Amish community. I don't want you to think I don't care for you, because I do. But you have to know what you're doing and what it means." He stroked the back of Eli's hand with his fingers. "And you have to tell me."

Eli looked up from the table and into Geoff's eyes. "Tell you what?"

"You have to say the words. You have to tell me what you're feeling, what you think you're feeling. I have to know that you aren't confused, that you'll be happy being with me, that this is what you want. You've been away from the Amish community for a little over a month, and I just need you to think about what it is that you truly want."

"Are you telling me 'no'?"

Geoff shook his head and continued stroking Eli's hand. "I'm telling you that you need to be sure. I know what I want. I really do, but I need to make sure you know what you want, because you are the one with the most to lose."

Eli's eyes cleared, and his face hardened into a fierce look Geoff had never seen before. "Do you think I don't know my own mind? Or what it is I'm feeling? That I'm some ignorant kid who doesn't know his own mind enough to know what he wants?"

Geoff lowered his eyes slightly. "No, but I care about you too much to hurt you." This wasn't going the way he expected, but at least Eli was listening. He kept stroking Eli's hand, wanting some sort of contact between them.

Finally Geoff said, "Let's head back to the truck. I packed a picnic lunch, and afterward we can ride the horses into the park." Eli just nodded and started to get up. Geoff reached for him, bringing their faces close together and then kissing him ever so gently before backing away again.

"You kissed me." Eli smiled as he touched his lips with his finger. "A girl kissed me once a few years ago."

"Did you like it when she kissed you?"

Eli smirked. "It certainly didn't feel like that."

The little Amish smartass. Geoff raised his eyebrows. "Like what?"

"Like the fireworks I saw once from our farm." Geoff couldn't help smiling at Eli's description of a simple kiss, not that he'd disagree. They mounted the horses and headed back along the beach, smiling at each other like kids who had just discovered ice cream. When they reached the truck, they watered the horses again and led them into the trailer. The sky was looking darker, and they decided to forego a ride in the park and just have lunch and head back to the farm.

Geoff got out the food while Eli made sure the horses had hay and treats. By the time the horses were settled, the picnic was laid out, and they sat down at the table.

"Geoff, there's something I need to tell you. Amish men do not court lightly or frivolously."

"I didn't think you did." Geoff handed him a sandwich and a container of fresh fruit.

Eli took a bite and set the sandwich on his plate. "About four years ago, I had a crush on Adam, a boy from the neighboring farm. He's a friend, and we helped each other with chores. It was then that I realized I was different but didn't realize there were other people like me. I thought it was the devil or something, and I tried to pray it away, wish it away, anything so I could be like everyone else."

Geoff opened a Coke and handed it to Eli, who looked at the can funny, sipped it, and smiled.

"I started reading what the Bible said about it, but that just confused me more. So I decided never to act on my feelings and to just push them away. But all I did was retreat into work and away from others. When you're my age, most social occasions are designed for courting, so I avoided them and remained behind to work."

"You must have felt all alone."

"I did and I have, until I met you and Len and realized that there are other people like me and they can be loved for who they are. What's amazing to me is that I'm not alone." Eli took a deep breath and released it. "Geoff, I'm Elijah Henninger, and I'm gay."

Geoff stroked Eli's cheek, and they smiled at each other as Eli leaned into the touch.

The wind started to pick up, drawing Geoff's attention. "I'm sorry, but I think we need to get going."

Eli got right up from the table and started packing away their half-eaten lunch as Geoff started hauling things into the truck. Geoff checked on the horses one last time and then pulled out of the parking lot and out of the park. Ten minutes later, they turned east off Lakeshore Drive and headed toward the farm with Geoff driving as fast as he dared. He pressed the speed dial on his phone and handed it to Eli. "Len should answer. Tell him we're on our way and ask for help unloading the horses as soon as we arrive."

He heard Eli talking to Len as he concentrated on driving through the wind that was buffeting the trailer.

They pulled into the yard as lightning flashed and thunder cracked loudly, vibrating through them. Geoff stopped in front of the barn and rushed to open the trailer. Len hurried out and helped them get Twilight out of the trailer while Geoff got Kirk out and led him to his stall. Len went back outside and closed up the trailer and ran in the house as the sky opened up.

In the barn, Geoff removed Kirk's saddle, blanket, and bridle and patted the majestic stallion's neck before leaving the stall and putting away the tack. Eli had just finished putting away Twilight's. The rain was pounding on the roof, coming down in sheets. "We should wait here until the rain lets up."

Eli came close. "What should we do 'til then?" He smiled, and Geoff slowly leaned forward, touching their lips together. Eli moaned softly as Geoff deepened the kiss just a little. Eli started to pull Geoff closer, but Geoff resisted, his mind insisting that they needed to go slowly. He pulled back, smiling into that angelic face. "It's letting up. We should go inside." Putting his arm around Eli's waist, he led him out of the barn, and they made a dash to the house.

The rest of the day was wet and rainy. Just before dinner, they put on raincoats and checked on the animals before retreating to the house once more. As the evening wore on, Geoff said good-night and went up to bed, climbing between the sheets, listening to the rain on the roof. He was just dozing off when he felt, rather than heard or saw, the door to his bedroom open.

"Geoff." Eli was standing in the doorway, dressed in pajamas. Slowly the door closed, and he felt Eli's weight on the bed as he joined him under the covers. Geoff pulled him close, Eli's warmth and scent and the sound of his breathing lulling him into a deep, happy sleep. This was what he'd been missing all those years: the closeness, the real intimacy, the sweet thought that Eli was here because he cared, and the love.

Geoff was such a goner.

CHAPTER 9

GEOFF sat in his office, head lost in the clouds, his thoughts on Eli rather than the ledgers and accounts, where they should be. Outside, the early June sun was shining. The windows were open, with a wonderful breeze blowing through the house. He should be content and happy, he really should, but he was miserable. In the last week, he'd picked up a summer cold from somewhere, and the damn thing wouldn't go away. Len had confined him to the house, and he'd reluctantly agreed because they didn't need the rest of the crew getting sick as well. Outside he could hear all the farm activity going on around him, and it made him restless.

A cough wracked his frame, and he closed the ledger and turned off the computer. There was no way he was getting anything done anyway. Giving up on work, he left the office and turned on the television, lying on the sofa in the living room after closing the curtains. All that was on were stupid daytime talk shows, so he quickly gave up, turned the television back off, and dragged himself upstairs to bed.

The cool sheets felt good as he climbed into the bed that felt huge without Eli there next to him. Except for the last few days, Eli had been sleeping with him almost every night. He would get ready for bed and come into Geoff's room, joining him under the covers. Eli always wore his cotton pajamas to bed, while Geoff generally wore sleep pants. Every night, they would kiss and hold one another, but Geoff made no move to go any further. That was strictly up to Eli. He'd promised himself and told Eli the morning after he'd first joined him in bed that they'd take things as slow as he wanted.

Actually, the truth was that the two of them sleeping together this way was probably one of the most erotic experiences of his life. He'd had hot, athletic sex with very attractive men—pounding-each-other-into-the-mattress type sex—but nothing was more erotic than this wonderfully warm, kind, sweet, innocent man with a fierce fire just below the surface coming into his bedroom each night to sleep with him, that work-hardened body pressed to his, their skin separated by thin layers of cotton, his scent drifting into Geoff's nose each time he breathed.

Geoff's eyes became exceedingly heavy, and he closed them, drifting into a rough and disjointed sleep. He woke some time later, unsure of what time it was. He could hear people moving in the house, but his room was dark. He'd finally found a comfortable position, so he didn't move and let sleep take him again. Hell, he was just grateful that he wasn't coughing his lungs out any more. This time his sleep was empty, no dreams, no thoughts, just empty. A few times, brief images of Eli or Len crossed his mind, and sometimes he felt like he was swimming underwater, but then there was blankness and nothing.

He opened his eyes. The room was dark, and there was something over his mouth and nose. He tried to take it off, but he was too tired, so he left it. He could breathe anyway, so what did it matter? Turning his head, he could see someone sitting in a chair next to his bed, but he really couldn't make sense of it. Why was Eli sitting in a chair instead of sleeping next to him? He tried to talk, but his throat was sore and so dry he just couldn't. And besides, he was warm and comfortable, so he closed his eyes again and let everything slip away.

When he opened his eyes again, the room was brighter, and he could tell that the thing over his mouth and nose was an oxygen mask and that he was in a hospital bed. Slowly looking around the room, he saw that he was alone. *How long have I been here?* There wasn't much in the room, but lifting his eyes, he could see a digital clock that told him it was just after what he assumed to be eight in the morning on June tenth. June tenth! The last thing he could remember was going to bed two days ago. *I must have been really sick.*

He heard footsteps and turned toward the door as Eli walked into the room carrying a coffee cup in his hand. Eli saw that Geoff's eyes were open and he smiled, set his cup on the tray, and hurried to the bed, his arms burrowing beneath him. "I thought… you were asleep for so long…." The pain and worry in Eli's voice came through loud and clear.

Geoff's throat was so dry he couldn't talk, but he used the hand that wasn't attached to an IV to pat the back of Eli's head as he closed his eyes, enjoying the feel of Eli's arms around him.

"I see someone's feeling better." Geoff looked over Eli's shoulder and saw Len walk into the room. Len patted Eli's shoulder gently, but Geoff motioned that it was all right and continued stroking Eli's black hair with his good hand. He'd given Eli quite a scare, and he needed to be reassured. Len pressed the nurse's call button, and a few minutes later a middle-aged nurse with a caring face walked into the room. "Could you let his doctor know he's awake?"

"Of course, honey, just let me check on him." She put her hand on Eli's back, "Sweetie, I got to check him out."

Slowly, Eli got up, his arms slipping from behind Geoff's back.

"You gave us quite a scare, young man." She talked gently while she worked, checking his pulse, taking his temperature. "Almost normal, that's real good." She jotted it on his chart and then took out her stethoscope and listened to his lungs. "Those sound much better too." She took all her equipment with her. "I'll call the doctor; hopefully we can remove the oxygen. And I'll bring you something to drink." Geoff nodded and tried to say thank you but gave up and just smiled. She smiled back and left the room.

Geoff looked at Len, hoping he'd explain what happened and why he'd ended up here. "We found you in your bed with a high fever, sweating up a storm, and brought you to the emergency room. They diagnosed pneumonia right away and got you on antibiotics and oxygen. That was almost two days ago."

The nurse came in again and took off the mask before turning off the oxygen. "If you have any trouble breathing, you just press the button right away." Then she left a glass of ice chips on the tray. Eli came right over, sat on the edge of the bed, and picked up the cup. He put a piece of ice to Geoff's lips. The coolness felt good, and the water slid down Geoff's throat. The first swallow felt like the walls of his throat were grinding together. Against his better judgment, he swallowed again. The pain was still there but not near as bad.

Eli leaned forward and kissed his still-parched lips. Geoff saw Len's expression widen, but Len said nothing, just smiled a little.

"I..." *God, talking hurt his throat,* "woke up and saw Eli sleeping in the chair." The last of the ice chip melted, and Eli gave him another one.

"You saw me?" Geoff nodded. "But you never moved all night."

99

"I just woke up for a few minutes, I think, and then fell back to sleep." Eli was hugging him again. "I'm sorry I scared you." Talking was becoming easier, but he didn't want to push it.

Len stood up. "I need to get back to the farm, but I'll stop by this afternoon after you've seen the doctor, and you can tell me what he says and when they expect to release you." Geoff lifted his hand and Len took it, gripping it carefully. "You gave us quite a scare, son, but I'm glad you're all right. I'll leave you in capable hands." Len had only called him son a few times over the years and always when he was worried or scared for him. Geoff pulled on his hand, releasing Eli, and Len leaned over the bed, giving him a hug. "I'll see you this afternoon." Len then straightened up and quietly left the room, his footsteps fading as he walked down the hall.

"Have you been here the entire time?" Geoff was starting to tire and he yawned.

Eli nodded. "Most of the time, anyway. Len took me home with him yesterday afternoon for a while, but I pestered him and he brought me back last night." Eli started to sit in the chair, but Geoff patted the edge of the bed and Eli sat there instead.

"When I woke up, I wondered why you were sitting in a chair next to the bed, but I didn't have the energy to try to figure it out." Geoff yawned again and felt his eyelids getting heavy.

"You should sleep."

"So should you." Geoff scooted over on the bed and made room.

"I can't do that; I might hurt you." Eli started to get up.

"Shhh… I'll be fine." Two shoes hit the floor, and then Eli was resting next to him, his head on Geoff's shoulder. Regardless of how tired he was and the fact that he was in a hospital bed, his body reacted immediately, and he had to move so Eli wouldn't feel his arousal. After getting comfortable and thinking of unsexy things, he sighed softly, happy that Eli was here in his arms, and they both drifted off to sleep.

Geoff was having a lovely dream, the warm summer breeze blowing across their bodies as they held each other close, Eli's lips on his, the horses nearby, a huge shade tree above them, its leaves rustling peacefully.

"Well! What do we have here?" Like a needle scraping over an old record, he was jerked out of his dream and into a nightmare—or daymare. Opening his eyes, he was confronted by the frowning countenance of his Aunt Janelle. Geoff closed his eyes and counted to ten, hoping she'd be gone when he opened them again, but no such luck. Eli had heard her voice and jerked out of the bed, trying to find his shoes, his face red with embarrassment. Geoff reached out and took Eli's hand in his.

"Hello, Aunt Janelle." He saw his Aunt Vicki and his Aunt Mari enter the room, his Aunt Vicki putting a huge vase of yellow roses on the tray where he could see them before leaning over the bed and giving him a hug and a kiss on the cheek. "Hi, Aunt Vicki, thank you for coming." She stepped back and his Aunt Mari gave him a hug as well, and he whispered in her ear, "Couldn't leave her home, could you?"

Mari kissed him on the cheek and whispered back, "I tried." He kept from smirking as she stood back up. "I'm so glad you're feeling better. I was here yesterday, but you were asleep with a guardian in the chair the whole time."

Aunt Janelle had planted herself in the chair by the bed, looking like she was making herself comfortable. Eli brought chairs for the other two aunts, and he sat on the edge of the bed, by Geoff's feet.

"The flowers are beautiful. Thank you."

His Aunt Vicki smiled; the flowers had obviously been her idea. "Have they said what happened?"

"They told me that it was pneumonia, probably brought on by a severe cold, but I'm feeling better, and they took me off the oxygen this morning. The doctor hasn't been in yet, but the nurse said I'm doing much better."

His Aunt Janelle interjected in her usual way, like a buzz-saw at a symphony. "I'm glad you're feeling better, but what I want to know is what you were doing with him in your bed?"

Geoff could see Eli trying to disappear. "Aunt Mari, Eli has been here for almost two days straight; would you take him to the cafeteria? He's got to be hungry." Eli stood up, looking dejected and miserable. Geoff put out his arm. Eli came close, and Geoff pulled him into a one armed hug, whispering, "It's not you. I just don't want you to hear her spite." Then he hugged him close. "I want to kiss you, and I would if I could." He made a note to himself to be sure they talked after his aunts were gone.

Eli got up and gave Geoff a small smile. Aunt Mari stood too, smiling brightly. "Let's get you something to eat and have a little chat." Mari winked at Geoff as she and Eli left the room.

"So are you going to answer my question? Are you and that boy… together?" Janelle made a face like she'd just smelled rotten fish. Geoff rolled his head against the pillow and looked at the ceiling, deciding how he wanted to answer. "Well?" Her voice was starting to get shrill.

"The answer to that question and any question that deals with my personal life is none of your business."

"As your father's sister it certainly is my business." That haughty tone was trying Geoff's patience.

"No, it's not. My personal life is none of your business, the farm is none of your business, and Eli is certainly none of your business." Geoff turned to his Aunt Vicki. "I haven't had a chance to see Jill and Chris. How are they doing?"

Vicki's face lit up. "I think Jill's getting engaged soon, but I expect you know that, and Chris will be a sophomore in college."

"Tell them to come out to the farm sometime. I'll take them riding. You too—I remember you were quite a good rider." That got him a smile from one aunt and a scowl from the other, but Geoff ignored Janelle, concentrating on his Aunt Vicki. Geoff rested back on his pillow as his aunt told him some of the exploits she and Geoff's dad had gotten into when they were kids. Mari and Eli returned and Geoff patted the edge of the bed. Eli sat down, a huge smile on his face. Geoff guessed that Eli and his aunt had had a good talk. They continued to visit for the next half hour, and Janelle even let go after a while and joined in the conversation.

Geoff began to tire, and his aunts got up to leave. His Aunt Janelle said a quick good-bye and left while Mari and Vicki took more time. His Aunt Vicki gave him a hug and promised him she'd bring the family to the farm. Mari told him the same and gave him a hug too. "You know this isn't over as far as Janelle is concerned. She's just biding her time. She can be extremely spiteful."

"I know."

"Don't worry. I'll let you know if I hear anything." They said their final farewells and left the room.

The doctor came in a few minutes later. "Mr. Laughton, I'm Dr. North. It seems you're doing much better." He checked his patient's chart and then pulled the curtain around the bed, leaving Eli outside. He listened to Geoff's chest and felt around a little. "You're doing very well. We'll have the IV removed and some dinner sent up. You should be able to go home tomorrow, provided you don't do any strenuous activity for the next week."

"Can I go riding?" Geoff was anxious to restart their morning rides.

"Riding in a car shouldn't be a problem." He never looked up from the chart.

"No, horses."

That took the doctor by surprise. "As long as it's not too strenuous, and definitely not for a few days." Geoff nodded, and the doctor pulled the blankets back around him and pushed the curtain back against the wall. "I should be in tomorrow morning, and I'll decide then if you can go home."

"Thank you." The doctor left, and a while later they brought him a lunch tray. He was starved, and to his surprise, the food wasn't too bad. "What did you and Aunt Mari talk about?"

Eli sat back in the chair. "You, mostly, and your Aunt Janelle. Mari told me to not pay any attention to her, that she's just a bitter person."

"She is." Geoff continued eating, suddenly famished. "I didn't mean to sound like I was sending you away, but I didn't want her to be mean to you. She tried, but I wouldn't hear any of it." He ran his hand down Eli's arm. "She can be a spiteful, vindictive person."

"I don't doubt it. She has the same look that Papa gets when he wants to show us who's in charge."

"That's it exactly. Janelle is used to being in charge, and if people fight her, she schemes or bullies you into going along with her." In the back of his mind, he wondered what she'd do next.

Geoff finished his lunch, and the nurse returned to remove the IV and bring him some more water. Once she was gone, Geoff had Eli close the door part way to block out the noise. "I'm so sleepy."

"Then rest. I'll be here when you wake up."

Geoff stretched out his hand, and Eli held it as he fell back to sleep, thinking of how nice it was going to be at home, where he could hold Eli properly.

CHAPTER 10

GEOFF was restless, majorly restless. He'd been cooped up in the house for three warm, beautiful, summer days. He wanted to go riding and spend time with Eli, but mostly, he just wanted out of this house. He'd already brought the farm records up to date and finished computerizing all the accounts. But most of all, he was tired of sleeping alone. He hadn't been able to hold Eli properly since that afternoon in the hospital when he'd napped with him.

His last night in the hospital, he'd had to convince Eli to go back to the farm with Len instead of trying to sleep in the chair in his room for the third night. *Besides, now that he'd awakened, he'd doubted the hospital would allow it anyway.*

He heard the back door open and close and footsteps in the house, and then Eli's bright face poked into the office. "What are you doing up? You're supposed to be in bed."

"I can't stand it anymore, and I'm just working on the accounts, nothing strenuous." He actually held his hands up in a sign of surrender. His quiet, Amish, non-confrontational boyfriend had turned into an instant drill sergeant the minute he'd gotten home, making sure he took his medicine, rested, and obeyed the doctor's orders to the letter.

Eli's face became stern and then softened. "See that you do; I want you better." Those blue eyes twinkled with mischief. "If you're good and rest, I thought that tomorrow we could go for a ride."

Hallelujah, fresh air, a chance to ride Kirk, and maybe be alone with Eli. That was almost enough to convince him to spend the rest of the day in bed... almost. He was feeling pretty good, and his breathing was solid with no shortness of breath. "Okay, I'll take it easy, I promise."

Eli bounded over to him. "As long as you promise to be good." Then he leaned over and kissed Geoff, Eli's tongue teasing his lips until they parted for him. Up till now, their kisses had been soft and gentle, with Geoff as the initiator, but this was different. Eli as the initiator was stunningly arousing, and man, could he kiss. Geoff felt Eli's hand on the back of his head as the kiss deepened, and he couldn't suppress a small whimper. Eli's eyes looked like deep lakes as he pulled back from the kiss. "Remember your promise." If that was the reward for being good, he could be freakin' angelic.

Shutting off the computer and putting away the records, Geoff moved to the living room, turned on the television, and spent a few hours napping through the late afternoon talk shows.

Geoff was awakened by the scent of dinner cooking in the kitchen and the weight of someone sitting on the sofa. He expected Eli but woke to Len's brown eyes looking down at him. "Dinner will be ready soon."

Geoff nodded and started getting up. "I've been thinking. We used to raise a steer to enter in the county fair."

"Yeah, that was one of the things we gave up when your dad got sick. Why?"

Geoff squirmed on the old sofa, trying to get comfortable. "I think I'd like to start doing that again."

"Do you want to share with me what you're thinking?"

Geoff thought out loud as he told Len the outline of his idea.

"I think that's a great idea, we'll put it to him and see if he's interested." Len patted Geoff's shoulder and started walking away. "Oh, I found out that the Winters are looking to sell their pastures and fields." The Winters' fields were adjacent to many of theirs and would be a good fit for the farm.

"Find out how much they want, and I'll run some numbers to see how much we should pay. Then we'll decide if it makes financial sense," Geoff said.

Len smiled proudly as Geoff got up from the sofa and went into the office so he could start putting numbers on paper.

Dinner was quiet, but Geoff noticed that Eli kept looking at him and smiling, giving him an "I know something you don't know" look that had him curious. After dinner, Geoff insisted on doing something, so he finished the dishes and then headed up to bed.

He'd just turned out the light and gotten into bed when his door opened and a sliver of dim light shone into his room for a second and then disappeared. "Eli?"

"I'm here, Geoff." The room was so dark, he couldn't see much, but he felt when Eli sat on the bed. Lifting the covers, he felt Eli's body press and mold to his. The way Eli moved against him was different. In the past, Eli had been careful to shield his arousal from Geoff, but this time, he could feel Eli's considerable shaft pressing against his own. "I thought I was going to lose you, and I promised myself that if you pulled through, I was going to show you, show you how…" Eli's voice faltered, "how much I love you." The words were barely above a whisper.

Geoff felt his body tighten; Eli had just told him he loved him. He'd known for a while how he felt about Eli. "I love you too." His tone matched Eli's very soft and intimate admission, meant for his ears only.

"Why didn't you tell me?" He couldn't see Eli's face, but he could feel his breath against his lips.

"I was afraid I'd frighten you, and I didn't want to pressure you." Geoff expected a kiss but heard and felt a slap as Eli hit him on the shoulder.

"There you go again, thinking I'm some sort of fragile flower you need to protect." Eli's voice had just the slightest edge. "Well, I'm not. There are things I don't know and I may need your help with, but I'm not fragile and I don't need protecting, at least not from you."

To emphasize his point Eli crashed his lips into Geoff's, kissing hard, showing Geoff in no uncertain terms what he wanted. Geoff got the message loud and clear, returning Eli's kisses. His body was maneuvered on the bed until he was lying flat on his back with Eli hovering over him, kissing his breath away, that tight body rubbing and vibrating against him. "I want to see you."

"You want to put on the light?" Eli sounded scandalized.

"No, but give me a minute." Eli rolled off him, and Geoff got up, shuffling through the familiar room to his dresser. Finding the matches he kept there in case of a power outage, he struck one and lit a small candle he kept on the dresser. The light illuminated the room just enough that he could see Eli's eyes shining with reflected light. Geoff walked back to the bed and lay back down. "Where were we?" He gently tugged Eli back on top of him, and Eli leaned forward and captured his lips again, picking up where they'd left off.

Andrew Grey

Tentatively, Geoff slipped his hand just beneath the hem of Eli's pajama top, his fingers tracing the skin of his lower back. "Can I?"

The answer was Eli capturing his lips again and wriggling slightly on top of him, so Geoff slipped both hands around his back, sliding them beneath the fabric, and began mapping the contours of the strong back, learning every contour, every muscle, with his hands. The bumps of Eli's spine, the dimples above his butt, the curve of his shoulder blades, all slid beneath his hands as Geoff mapped what felt like acres of smooth, soft skin that he'd been longing to touch since that first glimpse weeks earlier. His body was pushing him to go faster, the desire ramping up quickly, but he tamped it down, keeping it under control, reminding himself that this was Eli's first time and he wanted—needed—it to be special, and that required patience.

Eli kept kissing him, and warm hands slid along his bare chest and ribs, Eli doing his own bit of exploring. Geoff took the pajama top by the hem and lifted it up, Eli pulling away from his lips only long enough for the top to slip over his head and off his arms. Then those lips were back, even hungrier than before, tongue exploring as their chests pressed together, the feel of skin against skin sublime. Geoff wrapped his arms around Eli's back, hugging him close, a hand cradling the head of dark hair, their lips nibbling on each others'.

Geoff sat up slowly, their lips parting on their own. "Lean back, Love." His lips slid away from Eli's, licking and sucking their way down his neck to the divot where it met his shoulder. He gently worked the spot with his tongue, and Eli whimpered softly into his ear. Geoff kissed his way down Eli's chest, tasting the smooth skin before capturing one of the hard bullets between his teeth. "Fuck... you have perfect nipples." Geoff nibbled and licked the perky bud, and Eli began to vibrate with excitement as Geoff held him in his arms. Eli's skin tasted wonderful: salty sweet with just a hint of sweaty musk.

110

"Geoff...." At least he thought Eli was saying his name—it came out as a soft gurgled cry of pleasure. He pulled his tongue back, making sure he wasn't hurting him.

Eli's eyes widened. "Why'd you stop?" It came out as a soft whine as he mashed his chest against Geoff's face, obviously wanting more.

"Didn't want to hurt you, Tiger." Eli squirmed as Geoff kissed his way to the other nipple, swirling his tongue around it before flicking the hard nub with his tongue. Eli began wriggling against him, his breathing becoming heavier, his whimpers more insistent. If Geoff had a fetish, it was for nipples—small, firm ones that jutted out just enough for him to flick with his tongue—and Eli's were absolute perfection. To make things even better, Eli's seemed to be really sensitive.

Geoff felt Eli's hands on his shoulders, and he was pushed back against the pillow, taking Eli along with him. Then tongue and lips latched into one of his nipples, giving him the same treatment he'd given Eli. "Yes!"

Encouraged, Eli nibbled a little harder as Geoff began vibrating on the bed. "Use your teeth lightly." Eli did, and Geoff thought his head was going to explode. "Yessss!"

He felt Eli smile against his chest as he switched to the other side, scraping his teeth over the bud, zinging Geoff with a jolt that went straight to his groin. "That's incredible, Tiger."

Eli swirled his tongue around the bud as he worked his hands beneath Geoff and down into his sleep pants, cupping his butt with his palms as Geoff lifted Eli's head and kissed him hard, flipping them on the mattress. With another kiss he shifted off to the side and slid his hands down Eli's hips, taking his pajama bottoms with them, pulling them off his legs and sitting back to look.

Eli was more magnificent than Geoff could ever have imagined. Pale pink smooth skin, dark patches of hair in all the right places, long meaty manhood arching toward his belly button, and strong, work-hardened muscles straining just beneath the skin.

"Show me what you like, Tiger." Geoff stroked the skin of the long, powerful, legs as he watched Eli's eyes get big as saucers. "What?"

"I've never done that. Well, maybe a few times." A sudden look that Geoff could only describe as shame crossed the angelic face.

"There's no such thing as shame here, not in this house and certainly not in my bed." Geoff leaned forward, kissing and licking the skin of his pelvic dimple. "There's nothing to be ashamed of when showing your love." He kissed down to Eli's knee. "There's nothing here that's shameful." He started kissing his way back up. "Nothing at all." His lips reached Eli's groin, and he ran his tongue along his length before wrapping a hand around the hot, silky hardness and pulling gently, watching as the foreskin covered the head and then retreated. "So beautiful." Geoff leaned forward, bringing his lips close to the full head.

Eli gasped, "What are you doing?" as Geoff opened his mouth and sucked him down. Eli made some sort of gasping noises as Geoff took him to the base, relaxing his throat to take everything Eli had. The salty tanginess danced on his tongue as he pulled back and then took him again, this time sucking hard, pulling him into his mouth.

"Can I?" Eli moaned as Geoff worked his hands under Eli's butt and encouraged him to move, and soon Eli was thrusting gently, moaning all the while. Geoff could tell Eli was getting close; his whimpers were becoming higher pitched and a little louder each time. That Eli was making these sounds for him was thrilling beyond measure. Eli started to shake as he tried to hold himself off, but the need was just too great, and he barreled over the brink, shaking and crying out as he spilled years of pent-up desire. Geoff swallowed and swallowed, not willing to miss a drop as Eli jerked beneath him.

"I've got you." Geoff talked him down, letting him relax back on the pillow, holding his body close. "You're so beautiful when you come." Eli's heaving breaths subsided, and he started to squirm, and then he got up and pushed Geoff onto the pillows, attacking him with kisses on his lips, neck, and chest.

Eli kept going lower. Geoff felt fingers circle his length, traveling slowly up and down his shaft. "Is this okay?" Eli gingerly ran his tongue and lips along the shaft and licked the head before slowly taking it in.

"Careful, Tiger." Geoff could barely breathe. He had expected Eli to be more reticent, but he was definitely turning into the tiger Geoff called him. He took more and more of Geoff into his mouth, sucking hard as he did. "Good Lord." Hot wetness grabbed onto him and pulled him in, Eli sucking on him hard before letting him go and sucking him in again. There was no finesse, but the enthusiasm was driving Geoff out of his mind. Pressure quickly built deep inside him. "Eli...." His climax shot through him, and that was all the warning he was able to give as he emptied himself down Eli's throat.

He felt Eli swallowing, but there was too much for him. Eli knelt on the bed, smiling, as he swallowed. Then he wiped his mouth and licked his hand. Geoff groaned—that looked so decadent. Good God, he'd expected Eli to be shy, and instead what he got was aggressive, almost wanton.

Geoff collapsed back on the pillow while Eli kissed him sweetly. "How long before we can do that again?" Geoff looked down, and sure enough, Eli was already raring to go.

Geoff smiled. "Okay, Tiger, lay down on your back." The bed bounced as Eli hurried to comply. Geoff positioned himself between

Eli's outstretched legs. "Your job is to tell me what you like." Eli's eyes widened as he nodded his head. Geoff spread the long legs and settled between them, sucking first one, then both of Eli's balls into his mouth. Eli immediately started making soft pleasure noises. Then he released the meaty balls and lifted Eli's knees, pushing them toward his chest and licking down his cleft.

"Geoff—"

"Do you like it?"

"By all the stars… yes." Geoff kept going, running his tongue lower and lower, slowly zeroing in on his target. "Are you sure?"

Eli threw his head back, whimpering softly as Geoff's tongue circled his opening before teasing the puckered skin. Eli went wild, thrusting into Geoff's face, breathing in ragged breaths.

"I take it you like that?" Geoff got some sort of unintelligible response and then began to tongue the opening in earnest, thrusting deep. Taking one of Eli's hands, Geoff placed it on Eli's length, and Eli began to stroke himself, whining and whimpering, as Geoff skewered him with his tongue. The muscles clenched, and Eli went stiff.

"I love you." Geoff shifted his gaze to Eli's face and eyes as he watched him come, his Tiger coating himself with white ribbons, telling him he loved him.

Geoff lowered Eli's legs back to the bed and stepped to the bathroom, returning with a warm cloth and towel. After gently cleaning away Eli's release, Geoff dried him and threw the cloths in the bathroom. Turning around, he saw Eli getting off the bed looking around for his pajamas. Geoff took Eli in his arms, stopping his movement. "You don't need those. Come to bed with me."

Eli nodded and Geoff guided him to the bed. They got between the sheets, Eli curling next to Geoff. The room was now quiet, and the sounds of the night encroached into the room. Cricket chirps carried through the open window on the summer breeze, lulling them to sleep.

CHAPTER 11

GEOFF woke to the warm morning light peeking through the window and the sweet feel of his lover lying next to him on the bed—his beautiful, sweet, hot, new lover. And with the light came a chance to see him in all his glory. Long strong legs with just a dusting of dark hair, a high, firm, dimpled butt, soft and smooth to the touch, and a muscled back, warm to his touch. Geoff rolled onto his side, and Eli moved back against him, spooning them together, Geoff's morning arousal sliding between his lover's cheeks as he stroked his smooth chest and abdomen.

Eli's head rolled to the side. "Morning."

"Morning, Tiger." Eli smiled as Geoff kissed him gently. "You feel so nice." Geoff's hand had begun to wander across his chest, down his belly, and along the pulsing erection. Eli moaned softly, shifting his hips slightly to give Geoff better access. "So beautiful; love those noises you make just for me." Geoff stroked again, rubbing his thumb over the head, and he felt his lover's hips begin to thrust just a little. Lying back on the bed, he nudged Eli to turn and lay on top of him, lips connecting, bodies touching from chest to toes, Eli rocking gently, their arousals moving and rubbing together. "My sweet Tiger."

Eli moaned and shifted, kissing hard, and Geoff petted and stroked, not able to get enough of this wonderful man who threw himself into loving him. Eli was moaning into the kisses, making soft mewling noises, and Geoff was making his own sounds, the feel of Eli's skin against him driving him out of his mind.

"Geoff, gonna...." Geoff ran his hands down Eli's back and over his butt, sliding a finger down his cleft, lightly pressing against his opening. "Geoff!" Eli cried out, throwing his head back as he spilled between them with Geoff following right behind.

Holding Eli close, Geoff soothed and stroked his Tiger down from his orgasmic high, kissing and loving the remarkable man. Sounds of movement in the house broke their reverie, and Eli started to squirm nervously.

"It's okay; just relax," Geoff soothed.

"But, Len...."

Geoff couldn't help smiling. "I think he already knows."

Eli's attention, which had wandered to the door, snapped right back to Geoff.

"We weren't exactly quiet last night, or this morning for that matter." Eli started to redden, but Geoff kissed him, sliding his lips over Eli's. "No shame, remember?" Geoff wasn't sure himself how he felt about Len hearing them make love, but he wasn't going to let Eli see it.

Slowly, they got up. Geoff grabbed the towel he'd used the night before, wiping Eli's stomach before he wiped his own. Eli picked up his pajamas off the floor and put them back on before getting a kiss and leaving the room. Geoff whistled softly as he went into the bathroom to clean up. He looked at the shower, and his mind flashed to an image of him and Eli beneath the spray. He had to push it away so he could finish his morning routine.

Eli was already in the kitchen, and Geoff could hear him and Len talking as he entered the room.

"Eli and I have agreed that you can go riding today, but afterward, you're taking a nap and resting. You can work on the books if you want. Tomorrow you can start some light chores." Len looked so serious, but then he broke into a smile and shook his head. "Sorry… I shouldn't be telling you what to do. But I hope you'll take it easy for another day."

Geoff held up his hand in surrender. "I will. I promise. Maybe we'll ride to the south pasture, check on that portion of the herd, and head back. I'll get my ride and help you out at the same time."

"Fair enough, but don't overdo it."

Geoff agreed, and they ate breakfast as Eli and Len talked about the day's chores. The guys came in toward the end of the meal, and everyone got their orders before heading out.

Geoff finished his breakfast and did the dishes before heading to the barn. Eli had already gotten his horse saddled and ready, and the two of them mounted and rode out. It felt good to be outside in the sunshine again. Kirk was itching to go, but Geoff had to hold him back. He wasn't sure he was ready for full-on galloping yet, and the path they were on was a little too rocky.

"I've been wondering," Geoff said. "Would you like to visit your family? You haven't seen them since you came here. I could take you if you like."

"I was going to ask Len if he'd take me to visit them." Geoff looked at his lover, trying to decide if he should be hurt. "I can't have you take me. I know they'd see the way I look at you and that would be trouble for them."

"I'm sorry." Geoff was terribly sorry that the way he felt for Eli was causing him trouble.

Eli pulled back on the reins, stopping Twilight, and Geoff did the same. Slowly Eli brought them close together. "No shame, remember?" The leather of the saddle creaked as Eli leaned slightly to kiss him.

Those lips touched his, and Geoff forgot everything else. The horses, the field, the farm, everything else faded away. Then the lips were gone, and the world began moving again, and his brain started to function. What Eli said made sense, because he didn't know if he could keep the joy off his face when he looked at Eli. He hated hiding, but he knew in this case it was Eli's only option, short of cutting all ties with his family, and that was something Geoff could never ask Eli to do. Then another thought occurred to him: what if Eli decided to leave? This was his year away from the community. But, what if he decided to go back? Geoff couldn't suppress the shudder of fear that ran through him.

Eli must have noticed. "What's wrong?"

Geoff pushed back the fear, not wanting to discuss this right now. "Nothing." He just couldn't bring himself to voice the fear— what if saying it made it come true? So he pushed it aside and kissed Eli again before continuing on their way. He rode quietly, deep in his own thoughts. *This is dumb. He's right here, and I'm worrying about what might happen instead of enjoying what I have.* The fear subsided, and he turned to smile at Eli. He hoped they'd be together for a long time, but he'd accept what Eli was willing to give.

They arrived at the south pasture, and everything looked pretty good. The steers were a little low on feed but had enough for the rest of the day. He made a note to be sure to have the guys bring more out before evening.

To his surprise, Geoff was feeling tired, so they headed back to the farm. In the barn, Eli shooed Geoff into the house to rest. "I'll take care of the horses; you lie down for a while."

"Thanks." There was no one around, so he gave Eli a quick kiss and then headed to the house. Geoff had just gotten comfortable on the sofa when the phone rang. He answered, expecting it to be a telemarketer.

"Geoff, it's Raine."

"Raine, it's good to hear from you. How've you been?" He hadn't talked to his friend in a few weeks.

"Doing well. Just trying to plan a vacation, and I was wondering if your offer to visit was still good? I thought I'd come in a few weeks if that was okay." Geoff pulled out his calendar to make sure there wasn't something special going on.

"Should be great. I'll put you on the farm calendar."

"You mean like birthin' time? Or milkin' time?" Raine mimicked one of the Clampetts. *When he got here Raine was so dead.*

"No, smartass. Like 'Geoff will be away from the farm for a few days to show his friend around' time. But I could make it stall cleanin' time or manure spreadin' time."

He hoped Eli would go with them. He'd have to check with Len to make sure they could do without both of them for a few days, but there shouldn't be a problem.

"You wouldn't," Raine said.

"Then be nice."

"That's asking a hell of a lot."

"I know it is, especially for you, but we'll show you a good time, I promise." Geoff was really excited about Raine coming to visit. He honestly had doubted that the man ever would.

"I know you will, and I'll call you in a few days with the exact dates once they're approved."

"Good." Geoff stifled a yawn.

"The early mornings getting to you?"

"No. Caught a cold that turned into pneumonia, and I'm still feeling a little tired sometimes. It's nothing to worry about. When you get here, I'll tell you all about it." Geoff reclined on the sofa, getting comfortable.

"Okay, if you say so." Raine sounded skeptical.

"I'm fine, really. Drill sergeant Eli keeps a close eye on me, making sure I don't overdo it." Geoff yawned again. "Call me when you have your schedule, and I'll start making plans."

The line went quiet, and Geoff hung up the phone, lying back and closing his eyes. He expected to rest for a few minutes but woke when his lips were kissed gently.

"It's time for lunch."

Geoff opened his eyes, and Eli kissed him again. Slowly, he got up and followed Eli into the kitchen. Len put plates on the table for him and Joey, who'd just come through the back door.

"Hi, Geoff." He smiled brightly.

"Hey, Joey. Lesson today?"

"Yeah, Len is going to show me how to jump. Just small ones to help my seat."

Geoff started eating as Eli and Len joined them at the table. "I wanted to ask you if you'd be interested in a business proposition."

"Me?" Joey looked surprised.

"Yes, you. The farm used to raise a steer that we'd enter in the county fair. We won some ribbons over the years, and I'd like to start doing that again, and I thought you might like to help. I was thinking that you and Len could pick out two young steers from the herd and bring them into the barn. You'd be in responsible for feeding, watering, and cleaning up after them. At next year's fair, you and the farm would enter them. Then they'd be auctioned, and you and the farm would split the proceeds."

Joey's face split in a massive smile. "Really?"

"Yes, really."

Len nudged Joey's shoulder, "After your lesson, we'll take a look at the youngsters and see if we can pick out two." Joey smiled and began eating faster. When he finished, he raced off to the barn to get ready for his lesson.

Once Geoff was done, he took a pill, told Len he'd do the dishes in a while, and went into the office, determined to get something accomplished. After spending a few hours working, he was tired again, so he turned off the computer and went upstairs.

Geoff closed the curtains to darken the room, undressed to his underwear, and flopped down on the bed, falling asleep quickly. He woke to his door opening and closing, and then he was joined on the bed. "Tiger?"

"Yes, it's me." He could hear a smile in Eli's his voice and he felt smooth skin against his own. Geoff rolled over to face Eli, snuggling close.

"That was a wonderful thing you did for Joey," Eli said.

"It's just a business arrangement." *A mutually beneficial business arrangement.*

"It's way more than that, and you know it. You could have chosen the steers and raised them yourself with little effort and kept all the money." Geoff's forehead was kissed gently. "You're a sweet man, helping Joey like that without him even knowing it."

Geoff pulled Eli close and fell back to sleep. He woke hours later feeling better and very much like himself. The bed was empty, and he heard voices in the house. Dressing quickly, he went downstairs to a living room full of people.

"Did we wake you?" His Aunt Vicki smiled as she gave him a hug.

"No, it was time I got up." Geoff looked around and smiled at his Uncle Dan and his cousins Jill and Chris. He shook hands with Chris and hugged Jill tightly. Eli came in a few minutes later, and Geoff introduced him to his uncle and cousins. "Who's up for a ride?"

"I hope it's okay. You said to come by." Vicki sounded tentative.

"Of course. Let's go to the barn and get the horses saddled up," Geoff invited.

Eli led the way to the barn, spearheading getting the horses brushed and saddled before leading them out to the ring. Jill and Chris hadn't ridden much, so Eli helped them learn to direct and control the horses. Geoff brought out Twilight for Vicki, and she mounted like a veteran, easily remembering skills she hadn't used for years. Eli mounted Kirk and joined the other three as they rode around the large ring, helping Chris and Jill.

Geoff stood outside the ring, leaning on the fence with Uncle Dan, watching the riders.

"I wanted to thank you."

Geoff turned to look at his uncle.

"I don't know what you did, but for a long time, I've almost felt like I was married to Janelle as well as Vicki; there were times I thought they were joined at the hip." Geoff noticed his uncle seemed more at ease than he could ever remember him being. "Last evening Janelle was spouting her usual crap when Vicki went off." Dan watched his wife riding around the ring with such confidence, a look of pride on his face. "She told her she'd had enough. 'Cliff was gay, his son is gay, and you'd better accept it.' When Janelle didn't stop, Vicki told her to go to hell, asked her to leave, and told her she could come back when she joined the twenty-first century." Dan smiled wickedly. "I can still hear Vicki slamming the door behind her—sweetest sound I ever heard." Uncle Dan was smiling to beat the band, just vibrating with happiness.

"I never understood why she was so mean, and why Dad put up with her all these years."

Dan's eyes widened. "No one ever told you?" He thought it over for a minute. "I guess maybe they wouldn't." He leaned in like he was going to tell a story. "When she was about twenty, Janelle met a man and fell head over heels for him. She dated him for a few weeks and then brought him home to meet the family. Unfortunately, the man she was dating was Len. He took one look at your Dad, and that was that."

"Holy shit!" Geoff couldn't help smiling.

"Yeah, she never forgave her brother for stealing her boyfriend, even though Len always said they were only friends and that Janelle was making a lot more out of their friendship than there was. To tell you the truth, I tend to believe Len on that one. Janelle sees slights everywhere."

"So that's why Dad put up with her all those years. On some level he must have felt guilty."

"Not that he had anything to feel guilty for. He fell in love. Len didn't love Janelle, never would. But yeah, I think he felt guilty because he was happy all those years and she never was. Even though that's her own fault too."

"Poor Janelle." Geoff shook his head.

Uncle Dan's face hardened. "Don't feel sorry for her. All the pain and unhappiness she's felt over the years she brought on herself. She could have forgiven and gone on, but she held on and became bitter and miserable." Then Uncle Dan's face brightened, and Geoff looked up to see his aunt riding their way, looking every bit the commanding horsewoman.

"What are you two talking about?" Vicki asked.

Geoff smiled. "Just gossiping." Vicki looked unsure, but Geoff smirked. "Anyone who thinks women have a monopoly on gossip has never been to a gay bar. Those queens will rip you to shreds." His uncle snickered, and Vicki laughed so hard she started snorting.

Eli, who'd put Kirk in his stall, joined them at the fence, watching the riders.

"Hey, Tiger," Geoff greeted. Those big blue eyes shone at him as he put an arm around his waist, pulling him close. Geoff saw Eli look at his uncle, but Dan didn't react at all, and then he felt Eli relax against him. It didn't get much better than this: horses, happy riders, and his incredible lover next to him, enjoying it with him, surrounded by people he loved.

CHAPTER 12

GEOFF lay awake, watching Eli sleep like he'd done off and on all night long. He'd slept some, but not much.

"What's wrong?" Eli's sleep-filled voice carried to his ears.

"I think I napped too much today." That was only part of the truth, but he was reticent about admitting the rest of it. That Len had promised to take Eli to see his family today scared the shit out of him for so many reasons. What if they didn't let him come back? What if Eli didn't want to come back? And the question that really seemed to hound his thoughts lately was: what if Eli did come back but wasn't happy? He could deal with the rest, but he couldn't deal with Eli being unhappy. He just couldn't.

Geoff forced himself to stop these thoughts. This was Eli's year away, and they had plenty of time to spend together before Eli would need to decide what he was going to do.

Eli's sleepy voice cut through his thoughts. "Roll over and I'll rub your back."

Geoff rolled over, not so Eli could rub his back, but so that he faced him. Then he kissed him, letting the nagging questions melt away. This was what was important, right here, right now. He saw those big eyes open, shining like beacons in the dim room.

"Love you," Geoff said before his lips pressed to Eli's as he moved his body closer, slowly rolling him onto his back, pressing his lover into the mattress, hands roaming, lips tasting. But it never seemed to be enough.

Eli whimpered into his mouth as he kissed and probed, trying to get a taste of something that seemed just out of reach.

He tried to ask Eli what he wanted, but that meant breaking their kiss, and he couldn't do that... not yet, so he listened. Small whimpers and moans guided him. Those pleasure noises drove him on, building his own desire.

Finally, he pulled away from Eli's lips, kissing down that neck, tasting the skin, slightly sweaty, slightly musky, but all Eli.

His tongue found a nipple, zeroing in on it like a flesh-colored target. Eli mewled as Geoff nibbled and sucked on one, fingers rubbing the other. Yes... more of those sounds, that "love music" Eli made just for him.

"Geoff, yes, that's so good."

That incredible body writhed beneath him as he lightly bit on the nub of flesh, and Eli's music changed, became more urgent, more needy.

Then he backed off, giving Eli a chance to rest as he continued his journey down that luscious body, swirling his tongue around his navel. He continued lower, skimming it over Eli's hardness and nuzzling the fleshy globes. Lifting his legs, he licked a path to Eli's most private entrance.

"Geoff...." Eli let out a small, involuntary cry as Geoff swirled his tongue around the puckered skin.

"Like that?" Geoff went further, sucking and licking the skin, listening as Eli's music built, the pitch becoming higher, the tempo more intense. "Love those sounds you make for me." Geoff's tongue probed the opening, felt the muscle relax, and he went for it.

With each lick, each probe, Eli made the most wonderful noises that made his heart soar. Reaching to the bedside table, he found a small bottle and coated his fingers. Eli cried out as slick, slippery fingers teased his skin, swirling at his opening. Slowly, Geoff pressed just the tip inside.

Eli pushed into it, wanting more. "Feels so good."

A bit more finger slipped inside as Geoff made small circles, the smooth channel gripping his finger like a vise. Pushing farther, his finger slipped inside. Curling it slightly, he searched, and Eli cried out as he found that hard bundle of nerves, stroking it gently.

"What was that?"

Geoff smiled, bringing their mouths together, "That was your body telling me how to love you, how to take you to heaven."

Eli's eyes widened. "Take me to heaven, Geoff. Take me to heaven."

Kissing him hard, Geoff rubbed the spot with his finger as he rocked their bodies together. Eli was mewling constantly, thrusting against him slowly. "Love you, Tiger. My Tiger."

Eli threw his head back, eyes wide as his climax overtook him, and Geoff felt him tense and then felt his hot, molten release shoot between them. "Love you, Geoff."

"Love you, Tiger." Eli's heat and kisses propelled him as he hurtled toward his own release.

Eli thrust his tongue deep into Geoff's mouth, kissing him hard as his hands grabbed his butt, pressing their bodies together hard, giving Geoff just the friction he needed to send him sailing, crying out softly as he came and coated Eli's stomach with his release.

Slowly, Geoff began to move, gently withdrawing his finger, lifting his weight off Eli, kissing his lover sweetly, wanting him to know how much he meant to him. Hands cupped his cheeks, bringing their lips back together, as Eli showed him that that his message of love was received.

Then his Tiger took over, rolling them on the bed, pressing him into the mattress, kissing him hard, that sweet body pressing to his. Then the intensity began to wane for both of them, and their pace eased to sweet loving. Caresses became gentle and slow, kisses languid and deep.

"My Tiger."

"Love you."

Geoff's hands moved in long caresses from shoulders to back as they settled down together. He felt Eli's weight lift off him and the bed shake as his lover got up. Then Eli was back, a soft cloth cleaning Geoff, caressing his skin.

"Do you think you can sleep now?" Geoff was already drifting off as Eli got back in bed, pulled up the sheet, and kissed him sweetly. The last thing he remembered was hands stroking his back.

Geoff woke hours later, having finally slept soundly, to find Eli still asleep next to him. Strange—the man was an even earlier riser than he was. "Tiger." He gently stroked Eli's back.

He got a soft mumble in response. "Day off, get to sleep." Sweet. He settled back on the bed, pulled Eli close, and let sleep take him again.

When he woke again, it was to Eli stirring and getting out of bed. "Where you going?" Geoff rolled over and yawned.

Eli looked puzzled. "To get cleaned up and dressed."

Geoff threw back the covers and took Eli by the hand, leading him to the bathroom. "I think it's time you learned how much fun cleaning up together can be." Geoff started the shower and stepped under the spray, gently tugging Eli in after him.

Squeezing a dollop of shampoo on his hand he began massaging Eli's scalp, washing the rich, black hair. If Eli were a cat, he'd have purred as he leaned into Geoff's touch. "Rinse your hair, Tiger." Eli leaned back into the water, and Geoff soaped his hands, washing all that smooth skin.

"That's really nice," Eli murmured.

"Isn't it? Put your arms up." Geoff washed under Eli's arms and down his sides, leaning forward for a kiss as soapy hands stroked him slowly. "Turn around."

Eli complied and Geoff washed his back, spending extra time on his butt and legs, sliding his fingers through to tease his balls.

"Geoff...." Eli turned around, his erection pointing at his lover. Geoff smiled and sank to his knees, taking Eli in, sucking gently. Soon Eli's legs were shaking, and he was moaning, thrusting into Geoff's mouth. "Geoff, can't... gonna...."

Geoff pressed Eli against the tile and sucked harder, wanting to taste his lover. With a soft cry, Eli came, spilling himself into Geoff's mouth. Eli's knees gave out, and he began sliding down the wall. Geoff pulled him into his arms and held Eli tight, kissing his sweet, sated lover. "You're so beautiful, you know that? The most beautiful man I know."

Eli slapped Geoff's shoulder gently. "I am not... women are beautiful."

"So are you, Tiger. My beautiful Tiger." Geoff tickled Eli's shoulder with his tongue.

"Stop that." Eli laughed and tried feebly to pull away, squirming and giggling. Geoff held that sweet neck. "It's your turn to get clean."

Geoff acquiesced and let Eli go, standing under the water as Eli began washing his hair. Those hands stroking his scalp felt so good, and he gave himself over to the sensation. Then the hands slid away, only to return again, this time rubbing and stroking his chest with soapy lather. "If I'm beautiful, then you're..." Eli stopped and thought, his hands cleaning, and then he broke into a grin, "a stallion." Eli's hand slid over his length, the fingers making him throb.

"A stallion, huh?" God, that made him hot.

Eli nodded, sliding one hand after the other down his length. "Yeah." The fingers tightened. "A big, strong, stallion. My stallion." Eli turned them around, pressing Geoff against the back wall of the shower, stroking his inner thigh, telling him to spread his legs. Fingers gripped his length, and Geoff moaned softly. Then he felt a hot tongue slide along his crease before teasing his entrance, and he started to whimper—a high, needy whimper.

"Eli...." The exquisite pleasure was driving him out of his mind.

"Relax, Stallion, it's my turn to love you." And love he did. Geoff was driven to magnificent heights by those fingers and that tongue—that hot, searing, tongue. Of all the partners he'd had, very few had done this for him, and it was driving him wild. He began to move his hips back and forth slightly, and each time he did, Eli gripped his length and pushed that magic tongue into him.

"Eli...." He could barely catch his breath as the pressure built, Eli's fingers pulling, his tongue swirling. "Hot... so good." Lights

131

flashed behind Geoff's eyes as he shot hard onto Eli's fingers and the shower wall. Eli shifted behind him, hands stroking his back as he regained his breath.

The cooling water signaled that it was time to get out. Eli turned off the water and opened the door, handing Geoff a towel, eyes dancing. Geoff leaned close, going for a kiss. "How was that for cleaning up?"

Without missing a beat, Eli quipped, "Enough incentive to get dirty again."

They dried off, and Geoff handed Eli the robe he'd been using. After a deep, sweet kiss, Eli left to get dressed.

Later, in the kitchen, Geoff poured himself a second cup of coffee as Eli finished his breakfast. "When are you leaving?" He put the pot back on the warmer.

The back door opened, and Len strode into the kitchen. "You about ready?" Eli finished the last few bites and got up from the table.

Eli walked right up to Geoff, putting his arms around his neck. "I'll see you later." He gave him a kiss, a hug, and even a grab before following Len out to the truck.

They'd been gone about ten minutes when Geoff started pacing like a cat, looking out the window at every sound. *This is ridiculous.* Chastising himself, he went in the office and began looking over the ideas he had for the Winters' place. An idea had been brewing. He picked up the phone and made a call.

"Hello, Frank, this is Geoff Laughton. Len told me that you might be looking to sell."

"Yeah, Penny and I are plannin' on retirin'. Why? You interested?" He seemed hopeful. Geoff knew that Frank and Penny had been having a tough time of it lately. The older man had had some health problems and hadn't been able to do all that needed to be done, so they'd had a couple of lean years.

"I think so. I have a proposition that I'd like to talk to you about. I was wondering if you and Penny could come for coffee now." The line was quiet, and then Frank came back on. "Penny says that'd be lovely." He could hear Frank smile as he used her words.

"See you in a few minutes." Geoff hung up, started a fresh pot of coffee, and put cookies and some of Eli's homemade bread on the table.

He heard the old truck before he saw it pull in the driveway. Poor thing needed work. Then he heard Pete coming out of the barn, greeting Frank and Penny. "Sounds like you got a problem with the truck, Frank."

"Yeah." From the sound of his voice, it was just another problem on top of many.

"You here to see Geoff?" Frank must have nodded. "I'll look at 'er while yer inside."

It was Penny who answered. "Thank you."

Geoff came to the door and ushered them inside, inviting them to have a seat at the table.

"Frank said you have a proposition for us about the farm."

Geoff poured them each a cup of coffee. "Yeah, I do. I'd like to buy it, but I just can't quite make it pay at the price you want. But I think I can sweeten the deal in another way. Rather than buy all the land and the equipment, I'm willing to buy all the land except the acre that includes the house and your tool and equipment shed. You could easily sell the equipment to make up the difference if you wanted."

Frank looked skeptical. "Why would you do that? You could just meet my price and sell the equipment yourself and come out ahead."

"I probably could, but this way if you feel like it, you could keep it and rent it out when folks need extra equipment during planting or harvesting. I don't need the equipment; I've got plenty." Frank and Penny looked thoughtful. "There's one more thing I'd like to do."

"What's that, son?"

"I want to hire you as a crop manager." Frank's eyes went wide. "No one knows more than you about rotating crops, building up fields, what grows best where, when to plant, and so on. Dad did all that, and to be honest, I did okay this year, but I'm not good at it."

Frank looked confused, "The reason I'm selling is because I couldn't plant and harvest the fields I have."

"Don't want you to do that. I want you to plan it all for me. I've got people who can sit on a tractor to plant and harvest fields. I need someone who can manage what should be planted where and help build up the fields. I've got probably fifty acres that need augmenting." Geoff stopped to let them digest what he'd said. "You've got a lot of good years ahead of you, and just because you can't do the heavy work anymore doesn't mean you don't have a lot to contribute."

Frank and Penny were smiling.

Geoff continued. "Now, I want you to know what I'm asking. With the addition of your land, I'll be planting close to a thousand acres, with twelve hundred head of cattle on another thousand acres. Your job will be to plan what should be planted where, what fields need augmenting, and so on, to help make sure I have enough feed for the cattle and some to spare. Take your time and think it over. Let me know what you decide."

Both Frank and Penny were smiling at each other. Frank leaned forward, cradling his coffee in his hands, "If you don't mind my asking, how are you gonna pay for this?"

"Dad was smart, real smart. He put aside part of his profits for emergencies and for expansion. So to answer your question, I'm paying cash."

Frank whistled but said nothing more. Then he and Penny finished their coffee and said their good-byes. Geoff followed them outside and saw Pete closing the hood of their truck.

"Should be okay now, Frank." Frank thanked him, got in, started the truck, and they left.

Geoff heard the engine purring like a kitten. "That was real good of you, Pete."

"From the huge smiles on their faces when they came out, you must have been real good to them too." Pete moseyed back to the barn while Geoff shook his head and went inside. He heard a tractor start up a few minutes later and saw Pete heading out with a load of feed.

Geoff cleaned up the dishes and went into the living room, sitting in front of the television. It had been a productive morning, but he needed to rest awhile—especially if he wanted to go riding this afternoon.

The television droned on, and he put his head back and soon dozed off, jerking awake when the back door closed and he heard Eli's voice. The man was bubbling over and seemed really happy when he bounded into the living room.

"How was the visit?" Geoff asked.

"Good. They were pleased I had a job and was doing well." The smile faded a little. "Papa didn't say much, which means he figured I'd be ready to come back home already, but Mama was happy I was working with horses and seeing new things. She said I get my curiosity from her side the family." Eli sat next to him.

"So the visit was good." And Eli had come back and seemed happy to be here. That was a very good thing in Geoff's book.

Len popped his head in. "Saw Pete in the yard. He said Frank and Penny were here."

"Yeah, I talked to them about buying their land."

Len looked confused. "I thought they wanted more than we were willing to pay."

Geoff motioned for him to sit down. "I reworked the numbers, reduced the price, let them keep the equipment because we don't need it, and may have gotten us a crop manager in the process."

"Crop manager?" Len looked like his head was spinning, "Explain that to me."

"You know that no one knows more about planting crops than Frank. I sweetened the deal by offering him a job planning our crops for us."

"He couldn't plant his own crops. How is he gonna plant ours?"

Geoff smiled, "Len, not *plant—plan* our crops for us."

The light went on, and Len slapped his leg. "That's brilliant. And he can either sell his equipment or rent it out to make up the difference."

Geoff leaned back and smiled. "Exactly."

"You think he'll go for it?"

They'd seemed pretty happy when they left, but Geoff said nothing and only shrugged. "If they do, we'll need to hire another full-time hand so we can expand the herd. I want to add at least two hundred head."

Len thought it over for a while. "Let's work out the details if and when they agree to the sale." He got up. "We brought back lunch for you. It's in the fridge."

A few seconds later, Geoff heard the back door open and close.

"You did it again, didn't you?" Eli said.

Geoff leaned in close, tasting those sweet lips. "Did what?"

"Helped those people without them knowing they were being helped." Geoff shrugged. As far as he was concerned he'd made a smart, mutually beneficial business arrangement, but the smile on Eli's face was just too good, regardless of how it got there. Whatever he'd done, he knew he'd keep doing it if it meant being smiled at like that.

"Come on, let's get you some lunch and then a nap so we can go riding this afternoon." Eli led Geoff into the kitchen and, after his lunch, upstairs to the bedroom.

After a short nap, Geoff went to the barn to find Eli working with Joey, cleaning stalls.

"Hey, you're up!" Eli said.

Geoff yawned and then smiled. "Yeah, ready for a ride?"

"Sure, we're almost done here."

Geoff turned to Joey. "You want to join us?" He got a bright smile and a nod. "Be ready to go in twenty minutes." They worked together to finish the stall and then got the horses saddled and headed out. Joey raced ahead while Eli stayed with Geoff. "Tell me about your visit with your family."

Eli looked over at him. "I don't want to bother you with it." Geoff reached over and patted Eli's leg. "Papa wanted to know when I was coming home so he could schedule my baptism in the church. He said that there are a number of girls who want to meet me when I get back."

"What did you tell him?" He could see a cloud cover Eli's usually bright face.

"That I wasn't ready to come back yet. He began to get agitated. He really expected I'd be ready to come back by now, and he doesn't take surprises well. I think he understands, but he's just disappointed." Geoff looked over at him as they rode, and Eli huffed softly. "I think he's probably angry and thinks I'm defying him— like maybe I kind of defected to the English world. He really made me feel guilty. But I followed Geoff's rule."

"What's Geoff's rule?"

"No shame." Eli grinned and urged his horse faster, with Geoff just behind.

CHAPTER 13

"WHEN is Raine coming again?" Eli and Twilight trotted up from behind him, easily falling into step with Geoff and Kirk.

"He should be here in a few days." Geoff watched as Eli chewed his lip, a clear indication that something was bothering him. "What is it?"

"Did you and Raine ever... did you love him?" Eli looked so cute, biting his lower lip gently, eyes holding just a touch of fear. Not that Geoff wanted Eli to be afraid or insecure, but it told him how much he meant to his lover.

Geoff shook his head. "No, Raine and I are friends. We were never lovers." Now it was Geoff's turn to be nervous. He'd never talked to Eli about his days carousing in Chicago, and he didn't know how Eli was going to react. "I had many men when I lived in Chicago, but not Raine."

Eli looked confused. "What do you mean you had many men? You had sex with many men?" Geoff nodded slowly. "Did you love these men?"

"No, it was just sex."

Eli reined in his horse. "Has it been just sex with me too?" The hurt look on his face nearly broke Geoff's heart, and he could feel a twist in his stomach. How could he explain the shallow, empty sex life he'd had prior to meeting Eli? How could he make him understand that he wasn't some sort of prowling pervert? Eli's own words came back to him: "Just speak plain."

Geoff stopped as well, turning to walk Kirk back to where Eli sat, looking heartbroken. "No, it has never been just sex with you. My life in Chicago was very different. I spent a lot of my time looking for sex in bars or clubs. I spent a lot of my nights in bed with strangers. It was lonely, and the sex was hollow and unfulfilling. It took me awhile to realize just how shallow my life had become. I had no idea how wonderful sex could be until I met and fell in love with you." Geoff reached across to touch Eli's leg. "With them it was just sex; with you it's making love—very different, very different indeed. And I wouldn't go back to what I had then for anything in the world." Geoff leaned across the gap between them. "I love you, and I'm sorry if my past hurts you. Looking back, I'd change it if I could, but I can't. The one thing I do know is that it's made me appreciate how wonderful it is with you; and it is wonderful, special, and thrilling."

"You mean it?" Eli seemed relieved, and yet it must have seemed too good to be true. "You wouldn't just say that to me?"

"Of course I mean it."

Eli's head moved forward just a little, those sweet lips touching his. Geoff wanted to pull him close, kiss him hard. Make love to him right there in the middle of the pasture, show him just how much he meant to him, but that was going to have to wait, particularly since Kirk was starting to throw his head, becoming impatient.

"I love you, Tiger. All those other things I did before I met you pale by comparison. And when we're done with our ride, I'm going to show you just how much I love you."

"Is that a promise?" Eli's eyes were dancing again with that same delight that always made Geoff's heart do little flips of excitement.

"Tiger, that's more than a promise. That's a fact, so let's enjoy our ride, and then we can enjoy our *ride*." Geoff winked, and Eli's eyes went wide as saucers. Geoff chuckled and flicked the reins, and Kirk took off like the hounds of hell were after him, with Eli and Twilight right behind him. *Oh yeah, the wind on his body felt almost as good as Eli was going to feel in his arms.* The thought drove him on, spurring his horse to let go and carry them across the field.

"Whoa, Kirk." Geoff pulled back on the reins to slow the horse, panting and laughing as Eli reined in right next to him. "Let's get back. I have something special to show you."

"Special." Those eyes sparkled. "Like a present?"

"Sort of, but better, much better." Geoff was really liking the look in Eli's eyes, sort of hungry, like he'd expect from his Tiger.

"Race you back!" Eli winked and spurred Twilight on, racing back across the field, laughing and calling as he went.

"Hey, that's cheating!!" Geoff gave chase, giving Kirk his head. The only response he heard was a whoop and a laugh. They raced across the pasture, Eli in the lead with Geoff catching up fast, but then they reined in the horses and walked them to the barn, laughing. The horses were unsaddled in record time.

When Geoff was done, he closed Kirk's stall door and found Eli leaning by the barn door.

Andrew Grey

"Took you long enough," Eli said, those eyes just shining. Geoff laughed, bent down, and hoisted Eli onto his shoulder. Eli's feet were pumping, that tight body squirming.

"You're mine now, Tiger." He patted Eli's butt as he carried him across the yard, into the house, and up the stairs before flopping him on the bed. Eli laughed and bounced. "If you want your surprise, get yourself naked."

Hands flew, and clothes dropped by the bed. Eli got naked fast and was soon lying on the bed, waiting. Slowly, Geoff took off his shirt and then his pants, climbing on the bed like a prowling cat. "Love you, Tiger." Geoff captured Eli's lips, nibbling and sucking gently. "Want to give you something special." Slowly, he lowered his body onto Eli's, warm skin touching warm skin. Hands stroked, lips explored, tasting, touching, loving.

"What is it you want to give me?" Eli was vibrating beneath him as their passion built.

Using his weight, Geoff rolled them over so Eli was on top, pressing him into the mattress, their lips never parting. "I want you, Tiger. Want you inside me."

Eli went still, his head lifting, eyes staring deep into Geoff's. "Are you sure? I've never done that before."

"Never been more sure of anything. I want you to make love to me." Lifting his legs, Geoff wrapped them around Eli's waist, and he felt hot hands stroking his hips and sliding across his butt. Eli reached to the bedside table and used the lube to slick his fingers, sliding one inside.

"Is this what you want?" That finger zeroed in on his pleasure center, rubbing and stroking the cluster of nerves. Geoff could only nod slowly and open his mouth in a silent cry as another finger joined the first, twisting slowly inside him.

"Yes, just like that." The fingers withdrew and pushed back in again, "Yes... that's real good, get me ready, Tiger. Want you so bad." Geoff was throbbing on the bed, ready for his Tiger to love him. Eli shifted on the bed and the fingers were gone, leaving him with an empty feeling. Then, with agonizing slowness, Eli pushed into him, joining them together for the first time.

Since Geoff had recovered from pneumonia, they'd made love daily, but until now, they'd never done this. They'd never joined in this most sensual way, and now they had. Now Eli was inside him, filling him, loving him. The stretch, the burn, followed by pure pleasure, was almost too much. Eli was inside him, his Eli, his Tiger.

"Is this okay? Don't want to hurt you." Eli's eyes were wide. "You feel so hot, so good around me." Eli sounded short of breath, his excitement palpable. "Feels like I'm surrounded by hot, slippery heaven."

"It's perfect; you're perfect." Geoff looked deeply into Eli's eyes as he started to move, slowly and carefully at first, and then with increasing confidence. Eli experimented with different tempos and angles until Geoff thought the top of his head was going to explode. Every movement, every touch had him soaring. Then Eli bent forward and took one of his nipples between his teeth and sucked hard, sending him flying, and Geoff came in ribbons on his stomach. "*Tiger!*" Every muscle in his body clenched, and he felt Eli's own release fill him with liquid heat.

Eli collapsed on top of him, breathing hard, and Geoff held him close as he gasped for air. Eli relaxed, his breathing evening out as he slipped from Geoff's body. "Was I okay?"

"Tiger, you were magnificent." Geoff brought them together in a powerful kiss, using his lips and tongue instead of his voice to tell Eli just how much meant to him. Geoff knew that he'd thrown his innocent lover with his confession about his exploits before meeting Eli, and he desperately needed to reassure him. Eli was quickly

143

becoming very important to him, and he wasn't about to take any chances with hurting him.

"Are you sure I'm enough for you? That you won't get tired of me?"

Geoff hated that he could hear the doubt and that touch of fear in Eli's voice. He rolled them on the bed. "You are more than enough for me. In fact, I just hope I can keep up with you." They kissed happily, Geoff brushing the hair out of Eli's eyes. "And I might get tired of you, in eighty or ninety years, but I think I'll risk it." Geoff smiled. "How about you? I'm the only person you've ever been with. Can you be satisfied with that?"

Now it was Eli's turn to smile. "I'm willing to try."

"Oh, you are, huh?" Geoff began tickling his ribs, and Eli tried to squirm away and guard his sides as he laughed.

"Geoff," Eli was giggling and wiggling as he was tickled. Geoff let up, and Eli used the reprieve to tickle back, and soon both of them were rolling and laughing.

A firm knock on the door downstairs interrupted their fun. Geoff pulled on his pants, kissed Eli quickly, and grabbed his shirt, buttoning it as he raced down the stairs. "Just a minute!" He reached the door to see Frank Winters standing on his back step, looking worried. "Frank, come in."

Slowly, the older man climbed the steps and walked into the kitchen, looking nervous and very uncomfortable.

"What is it? You look upset," Geoff said.

Frank looked at the floor. "You know that we've been friends with your dad and Len for years." Geoff nodded. "But I don't think I can sell you the farm. It wouldn't be right."

"Wouldn't be right? I don't understand." Geoff pulled out a chair. "Sit down and tell me what's going on."

"I...." Frank's discomfort increased before his eyes.

"Frank, just tell me what's going on." Geoff sat down and waited for Frank to do the same.

"I got a call yesterday from Penny's sister, who told us we were selling the farm to...." Frank swallowed hard. "I can't even say it. She said were selling the farm to someone who was sleeping with a child."

It took a second for the words to sink in. "*What*?" Geoff's mouth hung open. "And you think I'm...." Geoff stood up so fast the chair tipped over backward. "That you'd believe such nonsense is disgusting." Geoff could barely control his temper. Frank looked down at the table, immensely uncomfortable. Geoff took a deep breath to calm his nerves, and he heard Eli enter the kitchen.

"Is everything okay? I heard raised voices," Eli said.

"Yes, I just got excited. Frank, I want you to meet Eli." Geoff watched as Frank's eyes went wide for a second before shaking hands with Eli.

"Good to meet you, Frank." Then Eli turned to Geoff. "There're some things I need to finish. It was nice to meet you." Eli shook hands with Frank one last time before heading out toward the barn.

Frank had the grace to look embarrassed. "Is he the...?"

"What, Frank? The man I'm involved with? Yes, and he's no child. He's almost twenty." Geoff couldn't keep the agitation out of his voice.

Frank stood, looking extremely contrite. "I'm sorry, Geoff. I should have talked to you to find out if what I heard was true. I really should have known better than to take idle gossip at face value, and for that I'm sorry." Frank got ready to leave. "Before Penny's sister called, we'd decided to accept your offer on the farm; that is, if you're still willing to buy the land. And for the record, I'd be happy to work with for you as your crop manager."

Frank extended his hand, and Geoff shook it, sealing their deal. "Don't worry about it. If I'd heard something like that about someone, I'd have thought twice about doing business with them too. I'm just glad we got it cleared up."

"Me too." Frank got up to go. "I'm sorry. I should have known better than to listen to Penny's sister. She always had a big mouth." Frank thanked Geoff again for understanding and then said his good-byes.

Geoff watched him go, wondering how that rumor had gotten started. Living outside a small town did have its advantages. Everyone tended to help one another, and everyone knew everyone else. But that was also the root of the problem: everyone knew or thought they knew what was going on, and people tended to talk. An innocent comment could easily get blown out of proportion and twisted with each retelling. He was just glad Eli hadn't heard the ridiculous rumor.

Getting up from the table, he went outside and down to the barn. There was plenty to do in order to make sure they could take time off for Raine's visit. Geoff had promised Len that the barn would be organized and the stalls cleaned.

He found Eli already hard at work. Half the stalls had been cleaned, and he was working on one when Geoff found him. "Want me to help?"

Eli smiled. "I won't turn you down, but the tack room needs organizing, and I'm not sure how you want it done." He scooped soiled straw into a wheelbarrow.

"Then I'll get busy in there and help you with the stalls when I'm done." Geoff headed to the tack room, spending the next few hours making sure all the tack was organized and put away properly.

When he was through, he looked for Eli and found him finishing up the last of the stalls. He couldn't help himself; he watched as Eli finished laying straw in the stall, his muscles stretching and flexing as he lugged the bale.

"Do you enjoy watching me work?"

"I love watching you do just about everything." Geoff stepped into the stall and helped spread the straw. "It's going to be fun having Raine visit."

"Do you think he'll like me?"

"I know he will. Hell, he'll be jealous... he'll want you for himself." Geoff laughed softly as they finished the stall. "We should think of some things to do while he's here. Things you'd like to do too."

"Don't you want to spend time with your friend alone?" Eli was biting his lower lip again.

"I want to spend time with my lover and my friend together. I thought in addition to riding, we could go boating on Lake Michigan, maybe go back to the state park for some hiking and swimming, if Raine's up to it. What do you think?"

Eli shut the door on the now-clean stall. "I think we'll have a lot of fun. I was wondering... does Raine know how to ride?" Geoff shook his head, and Eli smiled mischievously. "That should be interesting, teaching a city boy how to ride."

Geoff smiled in return and extended his hand, taking Eli's in his and walking back to the house.

CHAPTER 14

GEOFF heard a car pull into the drive in front of the house. Without hesitating, he raced out the front door and down the steps, reaching Raine's car almost before it had stopped. "Raine!"

The car door opened and Raine stepped out, immediately engulfed in a hug that was returned with equal gusto.

"God, it's good to see you. How was the drive?"

"Long and tiring. I need a drink." That was the Raine he knew and loved.

"Come on inside, and we'll get you fixed up." Geoff went around to the back of the car. "Pop the trunk, and I'll help with your stuff." He heard a click, and the trunk opened. "Jesus Christ, how long are you staying, a month?" The trunk was so packed with luggage, he expected the suitcases to come flying out at him any second. "God, it looks like you packed everything you own."

"Well, I wasn't sure what I was going to need out here on the farm."

Geoff shook his head in bewilderment as he grabbed the two suitcases, and Raine took the remaining bags, closing the trunk and following him in the house.

"This is really nice." Raine had set down his bags, looking around the room. "Comfortable and homey—not at all what I was expecting."

"And what, pray tell, were you expecting?" Geoff folded his hands over his chest, smirking as he waited for Raine's answer.

"I don't know, maybe deer heads on the walls and animal skins on the floor. Certainly not leather sofas and huge comfortable chairs." Raine actually seemed impressed. "And I certainly wasn't expecting a huge flat-screen television."

Geoff rolled his eyes. "We have all the necessities here, including satellite television. But this time of year, we're outside most of the day." He led Raine upstairs to the last empty bedroom. "We'll put you in here." Geoff set the bags near the dresser. "The bathroom is just down the hall." He looked Raine over. "You might want to change." He tried to keep the amusement off his face, but failed miserably.

Raine was wearing a pair of Armani jeans and a thin, low-cut shirt decorated with wings and emblazoned with Armani Exchange across the front. "What, this isn't good enough?"

"We're going riding, not to a fashion parade. Basic jeans and a T-shirt will do. I'll loan you a pair of chaps."

Raine's face broke into a wicked smile. "Oooooh, chaps."

Geoff ignored the obvious sexual overtone. "The seam on the inside leg of the jeans will rub your skin raw, the chaps stop that from happening. And these are anything but sexy." Geoff stopped a minute—maybe they could be. He'd have to see how Eli reacted to him wearing only a pair of chaps. It could be fun.

Andrew Grey

"Earth to Geoff."

"Sorry. Get yourself changed and meet me in the kitchen. Then I'll show you around." He shut the door and went back downstairs.

In the kitchen he got some sodas and a few snacks while Raine changed clothes.

Raine strolled into the kitchen, and Geoff handed him a Coke. "So when do I get to meet Eli?"

"He's in the barn working, but he's going riding with us." Geoff put a plate of sandwiches on the table. "I figured you'd be hungry too."

"Thanks. Is there some rum for this?" He waved the Coke in Geoff's direction.

"No. You'd never drink and drive." Raine nodded slowly. "Around here we don't ride and drive." Raine accepted the answer and took a swig of the soda, picking up a sandwich from the plate. They talked while Raine ate, Geoff catching up on news about the office, slipping back into the easy friendship they'd shared in Chicago. Geoff hadn't been sure if things would change, and he was relieved by how easily they picked up their friendship. Raine soon finished eating, and they headed to the barn, laughing and joking as they crossed the yard.

"How big is this place?" Raine craned his head as they walked.

"Right now, about two thousand acres. I'm buying some more land that'll add another two hundred and fifty. We have just over a thousand head of cattle." Raine whistled, and his eyes went huge. "It's the only way you can be profitable anymore. Smaller farms just can't survive unless they have some sort of specialty." Geoff opened the barn door, and they stepped into the dim coolness of the barn. The smell of fresh hay and clean stalls filled Geoff's nose. "Eli is probably with Twilight." Geoff led the way, opening the stall door. Eli was indeed in the stall, brushing the chestnut horse.

150

Eli looked up and smiled when he saw Geoff. "I'm almost done."

Geoff nodded and shut the stall door, leading Raine to the next stall. "This is Belle. She'll be the horse you'll ride while you're here. She's really sweet and incredibly good-natured." A big head poked out of the stall. "Wait right here." Geoff went to the treat bin and brought back some carrots. "Give her one of these." He handed the carrot to Raine. "Hold your hand flat." Raine looked at Geoff and then the horse before backing away. "She won't hurt you, just hold your hand flat." Geoff demonstrated, and Raine followed suit, holding out his hand. Belle lowered her head and sucked up the carrot with her lips and began munching away. "That's a good girl." Geoff stroked her nose. "Come on, she's not going to hurt you."

Raine stepped forward gingerly and stroked her nose the way Geoff had. "Her hair is soft." He kept stroking gently. "Is Belle short for Bellamundo?"

Geoff snorted softly. "No, it's short for Tinkerbell."

"I'll be riding a horse named Tinkerbell? Gee, thanks." Raine's eyes rolled, and then he burst out laughing. "A fairy horse being ridden by a fairy, how appropriate."

A stall opened and closed on the other side of the barn, and then Eli joined them.

"Raine, this is Eli." Geoff couldn't keep himself from smiling. "Eli, this is my best friend, Raine." Eli extended his hand, but Raine stepped forward, pulling the younger man into a hug. Geoff saw the surprised look on Eli's face, but he returned the hug and then stepped back.

"It's great to meet you, Eli. Geoff's told me so much about you." Raine was grinning as he looked between Eli and Geoff. "Anyone who can make him smile like that has to be really special. He never smiled that way the entire time he was in Chicago."

Eli moved next to Geoff, putting his arm around his waist. "Belle is all saddled, and I got Kirk and Twilight brushed." Geoff leaned to Eli, giving him a gentle thank-you kiss. "I'll finish saddling Twilight if you'll finish Kirk, and then we can go for a ride. You want to start him in the ring?"

"Yeah, then we can go for a short trail ride. I've got picnic things for afterward. I thought we could go for a swim. It's a hot one today." Eli smiled, and they looked at Raine. "That okay with you?"

"Sounds great. I'm already schvitzing like crazy." Eli just shook his head and went to saddle the horse, not evening asking the question. Raine whispered. "He's adorable, by the way."

Geoff looked at Raine seriously. "He's the sweetest, kindest, most loving person I've ever met. He's never selfish, works harder than anyone I've ever known, and he always puts himself last."

"So what's got you worried?" Raine knew him so well.

All of Geoff's doubts and worries surfaced. "What if I'm not good enough for him?"

"That's the cop-out answer. What's really got you scared?" God, he'd forgotten that he could never hide anything from Raine. The man could read him like a book.

Geoff lowered his voice. "What if he leaves? He's Amish and on his year away. What if he decides to go back?" He could hear his voice start to shake.

"You really love him, don't you? I mean, like… love him with everything you've got."

Geoff nodded slowly.

"Then the only thing I can tell you is make the most of the time you have. You can't control his feelings or if he decides to go back. All you can do is show him how much you love him and make the most of the time you have." Raine pulled him into a hug. "Your dad and Len had twenty years together, and it wasn't long enough." Raine tightened his hug. "If he goes back, will you regret the time you had or will you cherish it?"

Geoff knew the answer in a heartbeat. "Cherish it."

"That's your answer; it's that simple."

"Is it really that simple?"

Raine released him, looking straight into Geoff's eyes. "You can either worry about it, or you can make sure that if he leaves, you have as many memories to cherish as possible." His expression didn't waver. "Make the most of what you have. No matter how long you have it, it's never long enough. Just ask Len." Then Raine looked around, breaking eye contact. "I believe you have a horse to saddle."

Geoff did have a horse to saddle, and he didn't want Eli to suspect they'd been talking about him. He led Raine to the tack room, handing him the saddle blanket and bridle before grabbing the saddle and carrying it to Kirk's stall. Opening the stall door, he started the saddling process.

"Hey, boy, you ready for a ride?" Kirk bounced his head—he was definitely ready for some exercise.

"Why do you stand so close to him? Won't he step on your feet?" Raine stood outside the stall, scared to come in, which was probably a good thing.

"I touch him so he knows where I am and I don't startle him. And by standing close, if he does kick, it won't have much force, and he won't really be able to hurt me." Geoff continued working, talking in soft soothing tones. "Kirk is a stallion and very spirited, so I need to keep him calm. He'll only let me, Eli, Joey, and Len anywhere near him. He keeps trying to kick or bite most everyone else." Out of the corner of his eye, he saw Raine back further away. "Would you grab a few carrots and hand them to me?"

Raine moved slowly, watching the horse out of the corner of his eye as he got the carrots. "Just hold your hand out flat like I told you." Raine looked at him like he was nuts but did as Geoff said. Kirkpatrick lowered his head and scooped up the carrot, munching happily. Raine gave him another one and slowly reach out to stroke the long black nose. "He likes you."

"You mean 'cause he didn't bite my hand off?"

"It helps that you just fed him. He loves to have his neck stroked." Geoff finished saddling the horse and left the stall to see about Eli. He was finishing up as well, so Geoff led Belle to the ring. "Always mount the horse from the left side." Geoff mounted Belle to show him how it was done. "Now you try it. Left foot in the stirrup… good… swing your right leg over…."

Raine was now sitting on the horse, looking extremely uncomfortable. "What if she runs off with me?"

"She's not going to run off with you. Now pay attention. To stop, pull back on the reins. To turn, lay the reins against her neck in the direction you want to go, and she'll turn in that direction. To tell her to move, simply click your tongue and gently touch her ribs with your heels." Geoff clicked his tongue, and Belle started walking forward. "Try turning left." Raine laid the reins on her neck, and Belle shifted directions in a slow circle. "Remember, she's not a car. You don't get instant steering." Raine laughed and turned Belle in the other direction. "Good, now pull back on the reins." He did, and she stopped. "Okay, walk her around the ring while I go get Kirk."

Eli came out of the barn and brought Twilight into the ring and mounted. Eli trotted his horse in front of Belle and led as they walked around the ring. As Geoff expected, Belle followed right behind Twilight. Geoff went inside and got Kirk, led him to the ring, and after shutting the gate, mounted the stallion with practiced ease.

After riding in the ring for a while, Eli opened the gate and Geoff led Kirk out, followed by Raine on Belle, with Eli bringing up the rear. They headed across the field and toward one of the trails. "I need to check on one of the pastures, so we'll ride there and then come back." Eli waved his agreement, and Raine smiled. He looked like he was having fun and didn't care where they went.

As they rode, Geoff heard conversation behind him. He listened as he led the way to the pasture.

"How long have you been riding?"

"I was raised Amish, so I learned to ride as a child. We had a pony, and I learned to ride her."

"What's it like not to have a car?"

"You can't miss what you never had. The hardest part is that you can't go anywhere in a hurry, and sometimes people aren't patient when they encounter the buggy on the street. Papa won't even ride in a car. I had only ridden in a car once before I came here, and that was when I was just a kid with Mama."

"So what's it like? What do you do for fun?"

"Before coming here, my life revolved around my family. I worked with Papa or my uncle during the day. Some afternoons my younger brothers and sisters would play games outside the house with our friends."

"Did you go to school?"

"Yes, I went until I was about fourteen. Then I went to work with Papa, learning to make furniture."

Geoff listened while they talked. Some of what Eli was telling Raine, they hadn't talked about, and he found it interesting to hear how Eli grew up.

"I'm an okay carpenter, not anywhere as skilled as Papa, so I also work with my uncle at the bakery. I'm much better at that than carpentry. What is it like in Chicago?"

Geoff half-listened as Raine told Eli about Chicago, his attention focusing instead on the pasture. Large black dots moved across the field of green, grazing on the grasses. Geoff watched the cattle as they grazed and then took out his cell phone.

"Pete, it's Geoff. Get out to the northeast pasture and bring two rifles with scopes right now!" Geoff watched as a black dot lumbered around the edge of the woods, away from the herd.

"Is that a bear?" Raine was pointing at the spot, almost shaking.

"Exactly. Get off the horse and lead her back down the path." Raine followed Geoff's instructions, climbing down and leading her in the direction indicated.

Geoff got off Kirk and saw that Eli was already standing next to Twilight. "I'll walk the horses back down the path and stay with Raine."

"Thank you." Eli got the horses away, and soon Geoff heard a car door and then saw Pete hurrying toward him. "I'll take the first shot; you be ready with a second." Geoff took the rifle and steadied it against a fence post, aiming carefully, using the scope to line up the shot. Gently he squeezed the trigger, and the shot exploded. Almost immediately, the bear reared onto its hind legs, and Pete's gun went off. The cattle began to move away, and the bear went back down and stopped moving.

"Good shot, Pete. Excellent!" Geoff clapped the man on the back.

"You want me to make sure it's dead?"

"If you would, and, uh… you killed it, so it's yours. I'll call Fish and Game as soon as I get back to the house."

"What if there's a fine?"

"I'll pay it, don't you worry. Whatever it is, it's cheaper than a bear making lunch out of my herd."

"Okay… I'll call the guys to help get it loaded."

"Thanks." Geoff handed Pete the rifle and walked back down the path to where Eli and Raine waited with the horses.

"Did you shoot it?" Geoff nodded as he helped Raine get back on his horse, and then he and Eli mounted as well, and they headed back toward the house. Raine and Eli continued talking, but Geoff remained quiet. He hated killing animals like bears. He knew it was necessary when they threatened the cattle, but he still hated doing it.

Back at the barn, Eli helped Raine off Belle and led her to her stall while Geoff led Kirk to his. "I'll unsaddle them with Raine; you call who you need to."

Geoff nodded and kissed Eli gently before heading into the house. He called the authorities and explained the incident and that there were independent witnesses. They said they'd send someone out tomorrow morning.

He heard the back door open and then Eli and Raine came in. "Hey guys, I'm in the office." He got up and met them in the living room. "Are you ready for a swim?" Geoff sure as hell was.

Eli and Raine both nodded and went upstairs to change. Geoff heard the back door again and saw Len rush inside. Geoff explained what happened and that he'd already called it in.

"Are you okay? I know how you feel about things like this."

"Actually, I am. It threatened the cattle, and it had to be done. By the way, when you see him, tell Pete to expect a bonus. That was

157

one hell of a shot." Len smiled and nodded. "We're going swimming in the channel. You want to join us?"

"No, I'm gonna relax tonight."

Geoff nodded and went upstairs, meeting Eli in his room.

"Are you okay? You've been really quiet." Eli was there right next to him, and he took advantage, kissing Geoff hard. Then, remembering what he should be doing, Eli offered, "I'll load the truck while you change."

"Thanks, Tiger." The door closed after Eli, and Geoff changed quickly and headed downstairs. The three of them piled into the truck, and they headed to the park.

Geoff parked the truck just outside the park entrance where the Au Sable River meets Lake Michigan. The water was usually warm, and there was a nice current to swim in. Unloading their beach stuff and the picnic basket, they dumped their things on the sand and got ready to swim.

Eli had borrowed a pair of Geoff's board shorts. Raine pulled off his shirt and dropped his shorts, revealing his pink micro-bikini bathing suit, and then he tested the water before wading in.

"Is he allowed to wear something like that?" Eli sounded almost scandalized, and Geoff could understand why. There wasn't much to that bathing suit.

"Yes, he can."

"Isn't it a little small?"

"Probably, and if I know Raine, he wore it to see how people were going to react. He likes the attention." Geoff leaned close. "But I bet you'd look good in it." Now Eli really was scandalized, and he looked at Geoff like he'd lost his mind. "Not here, Tiger. But maybe at home, in my bedroom. You'd look real good one of those… or out of one of those."

Raine *was* getting a lot of stares, which he completely ignored. Geoff knew that was whole reason he wore the suit in the first place—that and the fact that he was out, proud, and man enough to wear pink.

"Come on, let's swim." Geoff needed to get his mind off the bear and his earlier worries and just relax. Raine was right, he definitely needed to stop worrying about things he couldn't control. Eli was here with him. That was enough, and he was going to enjoy it while it lasted.

He ran into the water with Eli right behind him, letting the current carry them toward the lake.

"I know that killing the bear was hard for you," Eli said. Geoff nodded as Eli's foot rubbed his leg. "I love that about you."

Geoff turned, definitely confused. "What, that I'm a wuss?" He sure felt like one right now.

Eli shook his head. "That you feel remorse for killing the bear. It means you care, even for the bear you had to kill to protect the cattle. It shows you have a kind heart, and I love that about you. It's sexy."

Geoff did a double take. "It is? You do?" He'd always considered himself a wuss. Growing up he'd never gone hunting and only learned to shoot because his dad and Len had made him learn. He'd gotten quite good shooting at targets but had always refused to shoot anything living. Today was only the second or third time he'd ever aimed a gun at a living thing. And to find out that Eli thought what he'd always considered a weakness was admirable only made him love him more, if that was possible. Suddenly this was the last place Geoff wanted to be, and he wondered how quickly he could get them home and upstairs into his bedroom.

"Geoff, you ready to eat?" Raine called from shore. God, the man was a shameless hussy—standing on the shore, wearing almost nothing. A group of teenage girls sat nearby, looking at him and giggling. Boy, were they barking up the wrong tree. Geoff followed Eli out of the water, his eyes on Eli's clingy-wet-bathing-suit butt.

They spread their towels and the picnic blanket on the sand. Geoff put out the food while Eli slipped on his shirt, and Raine reclined on his towel, giving everyone who wanted one a good look.

"You're a shameless queen, you know that?" Geoff commented.

"Well, duh. I could have worn a thong, you know." Raine propped himself up on his elbows.

"You'd probably get arrested."

Eli looked shocked, to say the least. "What's a thong, and is it smaller than that?"

"Yeah. Basically there's no back, and your butt hangs out."

Geoff was shaking his head. Eli actually shivered. "Not in a million years." He threw a towel at Raine. "Cover yourself before we eat." Raine looked at Eli and wrapped the towel around his waist. "Thank you," Eli said.

"Bossy, isn't he?" Raine looked a little miffed.

"I don't call him Tiger for nothing." Geoff handed out the plates and cans of soda. They ate and talked until nearly sunset. Then, after a final swim, they packed up their stuff and walked back to the truck. Geoff drove back to the farm, stopping for ice cream along the way.

The house was quiet when they arrived. Saying good-night, Raine went right upstairs. Geoff put away the picnic things, and after talking to Len for a while, headed upstairs himself. Walking into his room, he was greeted by a thing of beauty: Eli, naked, lying on his bed. The only problem was that his Tiger was already asleep. Geoff stripped down and quietly cleaned up before climbing into bed. Eli barely moved as Geoff kissed him softly before easily sliding into sleep.

Andrew Grey

CHAPTER 15

GEOFF woke to heaven—he must have been in heaven. The morning light bounced off a head of dark hair resting on his chest as hands slowly roamed over his skin and lips teased one of his nipples. Geoff moaned softly, kissing Eli on the head as he ran his fingers through the soft hair. Eli's head shifted until his eyes locked on Geoff's. Then their lips met, and Eli shifted, straddling Geoff's hips. "I want you, Geoff. I want you so bad."

Eli's lips were driving him wild, and Geoff hugged him close, their kisses becoming more urgent, more needy. "What do you want, Tiger?" Geoff let his hands slide down Eli's back, cupping that incredible butt.

"That. I want that!" Eli's back arched as Geoff slid a finger down his crease. "Yes... that's what I want... you!" Eli's lips crashed down onto Geoff, tongue sliding in, his Tiger taking what he wanted.

"You sure?" Geoff asked when he broke free. This would be Eli's first time, and Geoff needed to make sure that was what he truly wanted. The last thing he wanted was to hurt Eli or push him

162

into something he wasn't ready for, but his answer came in the way Eli was vibrating against his skin every time he touched him.

"Oh yes. I want you to love me."

Geoff hugged him hard, bringing as much skin into contact as possible. "I already do." Slowly, lazily, Geoff rolled them over on the bed, Eli's legs circling around his waist, leaving no doubt whatsoever as to what Eli was asking. Geoff reached to the bedside table, slicking his fingers with lube, using them to tease Eli's tight opening.

Eli moaned softly as Geoff felt the puckered skin, making small circles as he worked his finger inside. "Geoff...."

He loved it when Eli moaned his name—that he was making such incredible noises for him. Geoff pushed his finger deeper. "Feel good?" He curled his finger, rubbing slowly.

"Yes!" Eli cried out and pushed back against Geoff's hand, driving him deeper into that hot, tight body. Geoff pulled his finger away and added a second, scissoring them and slowly twisting. Eli started moaning louder, whimpering whenever he pulled out, mewling softly as Geoff pushed back inside.

Eli's body was so hot and tight, Geoff didn't know if he'd be able to last. The heat coming off him was almost too much. "You make me crazy for you." Slowly he withdrew his fingers and looked down at Eli, whose eyes were wide with desire, body shaking slightly, legs spread in invitation.

"Geoff, hurry, please." Eli's were so deep, so full of passion; it was the singular most beautiful sight he'd ever seen. Geoff leaned forward and kissed his lover hard as he slowly entered his body, watching his expression for signs of discomfort.

Eli's eyes widened further as his guardian muscle stretched for the first time. Geoff stopped moving. "Are you okay?" Eli didn't move right away, and Geoff began to pull out.

"No, I'm fine. So full."

With a small sigh, Geoff began pushing back inside, Eli's heat drawing him in, the draw so forceful he couldn't have stopped himself even if he wanted to. After what felt like a blissful eternity, his hips rested against Eli's body.

"Geoff, I can almost feel your heart beating inside me." Geoff smiled and tensed his muscles. "Geoff… you danced in me."

Slowly, Geoff pulled out, Eli's body tugging on him as he moved. Eli whimpered softly and then groaned deeply as Geoff pushed back in deep.

"You look so hot right now," Geoff said.

"I feel hot right now, like I'm on fire… for you." Eli reached out, his fingers sliding down Geoff's chest and stomach. "I want you, Geoff. I want to feel you."

"You'll feel me." Geoff continued his pace, slow and steady, making every stroke count. "You'll feel me when you're riding, when you're walking, when you're sitting at the table."

"Gosh…." Eli's breathing was deep and heavy, his eyes full. Geoff wrapped his hand around Eli's length and began stroking, moving to the tempo of their lovemaking.

"*Geoff*!" He felt Eli pulse in his hand as he cried out and came, body throbbing on the mattress as Geoff followed right behind, pulled into his own release by the near vise grip of Eli's body.

Slowly, reluctantly, Geoff pulled out of Eli's body, breaking the physical connection. After a quick cleanup, Geoff pulled Eli close. "Love you."

Eli rolled over, kissing him. "Love you too." Eli's eyes drifted shut, and soon he'd drifted off, with Geoff not far behind him.

Geoff woke to the morning sounds of the farm. He heard movement in the house and slowly extricated himself from his still sleeping lover's embrace. Dressing quietly, he left the room, letting Eli sleep. Downstairs, he found Len in the kitchen.

"Raine's going home tomorrow?" Len asked. Geoff nodded as he poured a cup of coffee. "What's planned for today?"

"Don't know. I thought we'd probably stay close, ride some, let him take it easy before he drives home. It's been nice having him here."

Len sipped from his mug. "I could tell. All three of you seem to be having a good time." He finished his coffee and put the mug in the sink. "Have fun today."

Geoff sat at the table and smiled to himself, sipping from his mug. He heard footsteps, and Eli came in, pouring himself a mug from the pot. "Why didn't you get me up with you?"

"You were sleeping so soundly, I didn't want to wake you."

Eli leaned to him, kissing his lips softly.

"I thought we'd take it easy today, maybe go out for dinner tonight, just relax," Geoff said. Eli sat gingerly at the table, and Geoff smiled. "You okay?"

Eli returned the smile. "A little sore, but it feels sort of good— like I can still feel you."

Geoff hid a grin behind his coffee cup. He liked that Eli could still feel him and would still feel him for most of the day.

"How in the hell can you get up so godawful early every day?" Raine yawned as he plopped in a chair. "God, the sun isn't even awake yet." Geoff got up and poured Raine a mug of coffee, handing it to him between yawns.

"I thought we'd take it easy today, maybe ride some and you can relax. Tonight we'll go out." Geoff stood up. "We've got a few chores to do. You can relax for a while if you want." Raine nodded and sipped his coffee while Geoff and Eli headed to the barn.

They spent the next couple of hours cleaning stalls. When they were done, they put their tools away and headed back toward the house. To their surprise, they found Raine leaning against the paddock fence watching the colt and his mother.

"How old is he again?" Raine asked.

"About two months."

"He sure is beautiful."

Geoff leaned against the fence, putting an arm around Eli's waist. "Kirk's his sire." They watched as the young colt ran and played around his mother. "I never knew how wonderful it could be outside the city." Raine turned to face Geoff. "I thought you were nuts for leaving Chicago, but I can see you were the smart one. You're really happy here, and you weren't there." Geoff tried to argue, but Raine stopped him. "Not like you are here."

Geoff's stomach rumbled loudly, and they took that as a sign, heading inside to eat.

After lunch, they spent the afternoon riding and relaxing until it was time to get ready for dinner.

"Are you two ready to go?" Geoff found Eli and Raine both in the living room.

"We've been waiting for you." Geoff rolled his eyes at Raine and led the way outside and to the truck, and they headed toward town, laughing and enjoying themselves. Geoff knew he was going to be sad to see Raine leave. He drove through town and pulled up to a familiar restaurant that had a view of the lake. After telling the hostess his name, they were seated at a table near the windows.

"Geoff, this is so nice." Eli was wide-eyed as he looked around the restaurant and took the menu from the hostess. "I've never been to any place like this before."

Geoff squeezed Eli's knee to reassure him. "Just have fun and be yourself." Eli smiled and opened his menu. Their server stopped by the table, explained the specials, and took their drink orders. Raine and Geoff ordered a glass of wine, and Eli ordered a soda.

They talked and laughed while they looked over the menu. Raine was the first to set his down. "I'm having the perch."

"I can't decide between the salmon or the duck. What about you, Eli?"

Eli put his menu down. "I don't really know." He seemed a little overwhelmed.

Geoff leaned close. "Do you want me to order for you?"

Eli shook his head. "I just don't want to embarrass you if I do something wrong."

"You won't, Tiger. Just relax and enjoy." Geoff leaned close. "There is nothing you could do to embarrass me as long as you just be you. Okay?"

Eli nodded and returned his attention to the menu. "I'm going to try the duck."

"Then I'll have the salmon," Geoff said.

The server came over and took their orders, returning a few minutes later with their drinks and salads. They talked and laughed together. Geoff kept an eye on Eli, who just seemed uncomfortable in an "out of his element, not sure of himself" kind of way.

"Eli, look over there." Geoff indicated a table with children. "If they can eat here, spilling food everywhere, you have nothing to worry about." Geoff squeezed Eli's leg again, and Eli finally seemed to relax.

The server brought their entrees, which looked delicious. Eli did have some trouble with the duck but acquitted himself well in the end. The food was delicious and very filling. The server inquired about dessert, but they all declined. When the check arrived, Raine grabbed for it and slapped Geoff's hand when he tried to take it back. "It's the least I can do to say thank you to both of you for making my vacation so much fun." The server returned, and Raine handed him his credit card.

"Thank you, Raine." After being nervous earlier, Eli now looked full and very content.

"Yes... thank you. That wasn't necessary," Geoff said.

"Yes, it was." Raine signed the check. "So stop." They got up and left the restaurant, saying good-night on their way out.

Outside, it was just getting dark as they walked down the street to the truck. "Hey fags!" Geoff looked around. "Yeah, I'm talking to you, faggot!" Geoff and Raine spun around as three guys came up behind them. "We heard about you." The three of them looked like just-graduated high-school football players, and Geoff was sure he'd seen them around town before.

"Eli, run to the truck." He heard a squeak and saw Eli back away out of the corner of his eye.

"We heard all about you. Is that the boy you been carrying on with?" Geoff didn't turn around and started to back away. The men advanced on him. One of them grabbed Raine, holding him tight. "We heard all about you. Seems your relatives don't like you carrying on with little boys either." The guy closest to Geoff pushed him to the pavement, and Geoff curled into a ball just before he was kicked in the side and leg.

Other people on the street stopped. "Someone call the police." A few seconds later, Geoff heard someone speaking into a phone.

"Let's get out of here!" The three of them took off down the street at a run.

When he heard the running, Geoff uncurled himself and tried getting up. His side hurt, but nothing appeared to be broken. It seemed his leg had gotten the worst of it. "Raine, are you okay?"

The people gathered around had helped Raine up. "Yeah, I think so."

"Where's Eli?" His leg hurt and was going to be black and blue for a while, but everything seemed to be working okay and the pain in his side was easing, thank God.

"I think he's by the truck." Geoff saw Eli standing near the truck, looking like a deer in headlights. They heard sirens, and a police car pulled up a few seconds later, sirens blaring, lights flashing.

The policemen got out, and Geoff beckoned them over. They asked all kinds of questions about what had happened, and Geoff told them about the accusation the men made. Understandably, the police were very interested, and they walked to the truck and spoke briefly with Eli before finishing up their questions. Finally, after what seemed like hours, they were told they could go. Geoff asked Raine to drive, and Eli helped him into the truck.

The ride back to the farm was anything but joyful. Geoff was in pain and felt like crap. When they reached the farm, Eli and Raine helped him out of the truck and into the house. They found Len in the living room.

"What happened?" Len asked.

Geoff explained about the incident in Ludington after lowering himself into a chair. Eli sat on the sofa, looking at him.

"Why would they do that?" Len looked worried.

"One of the kids said that my relatives didn't like me carrying on with boys either. I think someone has been spreading rumors that I'm having a relationship with someone underage."

Len jumped to his feet. "That bitch!"

"We don't know it's her." Geoff didn't sound convincing, even to himself.

"That's just the type of thing she would do, though. Spreading lies all around town. Hell, she doesn't even need to tell lies. All she'd do is embellish the truth and let those busybodies take it from there."

Geoff was too tired to figure it out right now. Slowly, he got up, gave Len and Raine each a hug, and limped painfully upstairs to his bedroom.

The first thing he did was take something for the pain. Then he got undressed and climbed into bed. He heard voices drifting up from downstairs as he lay there, his thoughts drifting to his dad and then Eli. Tears came unbidden to his eyes, and he tried to brush them away, but more took their place. *Maybe I shouldn't have stayed here. Maybe I should have sold the farm when I had the chance. What if they'd hurt Eli or Raine instead of me?*

He was so deep in his self pity that he didn't hear his door open and close, but he felt Eli's arms around him, and that touch released a torrent of tears. "I'm sorry. I'm sorry." Geoff's body ached, he cried so hard.

"It's okay." Eli rocked him gently as he clung to him. "Lay back." Eli settled him back on the pillow as his tears tapered off and got up off the bed. Geoff half expected him to leave, but Eli used the bathroom and then got back into bed, holding him until he fell asleep.

Geoff had a rough night. His leg hurt, and he woke often, but Eli was there. When he woke in the morning, the bed was empty, but he heard Eli in the bathroom. Pushing back the covers, he looked at his side. His hip and calf were dark purple, and his leg was stiff and achy. Slowly he got to his feet, pulling on a pair of pants and shrugging into a shirt.

Eli came out of the bathroom looking almost as bad as Geoff felt. He threw on his robe, and after giving Geoff a quick kiss, went down to his room to dress. Geoff cleaned up and went downstairs.

Raine was already up and having a cup of coffee. "How's your leg?"

"Rainbow-colored, but not too bad otherwise." Geoff sat down at the table, and Len brought him some coffee.

Len sat down. "The police called this morning. They have the three men who assaulted you. They'd been drinking for much of the day yesterday. The officer said they were in jail and being charged with assault. He also said that when they sobered up, they confessed to everything." He sipped his coffee. "One of the boys is Frank and Penny Winters' nephew."

Geoff sighed as he sipped his coffee, having nothing to say.

Raine finished his coffee. "I've got to head out. Will you walk me out so I can say good-bye?" As they walked through the house, they met Eli coming down the stairs. Raine hugged him tight and said something to Eli, but Geoff couldn't hear it. Then he continued outside to the car.

"Is everything loaded?" Geoff asked.

"Len helped me this morning. Look, you take care and don't let this get you down. It was just a bunch of stupid kids who'd had too much to drink. Besides, you need to take care of Eli." Raine huffed when he saw Geoff's expression and smacked him gently on shoulder. "He saw and heard everything that happened last night,

171

and he's feeling worse than you. You lived in Chicago and saw things like this; he never has." Raine hugged him close. "Take care of each other. You truly deserve one another." Raine hugged him one more time and then climbed in the car, started the engine, and with a wave, pulled out of the drive.

Raine was right; Geoff had seen things like this before. Straightening himself up, he went back in the house. Len was making a quick breakfast. "Did you see where Eli went?"

"He grabbed something and headed to the barn." Len put a plate in front of him. "Eat first." Geoff acquiesced and sat with Len, eating a good breakfast. When Geoff had taken the last bite, Len shooed him out of the house. "Okay, now you can go find him."

"Thanks." Geoff headed to the barn but found it quiet when he got inside. Looking in the stalls, he discovered that Twilight was gone.

"He probably needs some time alone to think," Len said, patting him on the shoulder as he walked by on his way to the riding ring. Joey was already outside, ready for his lesson, a huge smile on his face. Turning around, Geoff walked back though the barn and into the house without even seeing where he was going.

In the office, he booted up the computer and got to work. He had books to bring up to date, orders to place, and real estate contracts to review. Forcing everything else from his mind, he got to work, stopping only for a quick lunch. At about five in the afternoon, he'd finished everything he needed to. He'd gotten the books up to date, reviewed the contract, and contacted the lawyer to schedule the closing on the Winters' place.

Getting up, he moved stiffly through the house and out to the barn. Eli was in the stall with the young colt, working quietly, making sure he was okay.

"Eli, are you almost done?"

Eli turned around, and Geoff saw tears streaked down his face. "Yes."

God, I shouldn't have left him alone so long.

Eli returned the colt to the pasture, tears still marring his face. Geoff stepped to take him in his arms, but Eli stopped him. "I'm okay, Geoff." He wiped his face with the back of his hand and got himself under control. "I'm done here. Can we go the house and talk?"

"Yes, I think we should." Geoff took Eli's hand and led him inside and to the living room, where he sat next to Eli on the sofa and waited.

Geoff watched as the tears started again, flowing silently down Eli's cheeks. "I don't know how to say this."

"I know what you saw last night upset you, and I don't blame you."

Eli wiped his face again. "It's not just that. I heard what they said. I know that your aunt has been spreading vicious rumors and lies about us." He sniffled, and Geoff moved to hold him, but Eli moved away. "People don't get beaten up in an Amish community, and they don't spread lies like that. They help and support one another." The tears started flowing fast, and Geoff felt his own well behind his eyes. "If talk reaches the community about us, my family will be shunned... heck, they might as well not exist to the rest of the community. My uncle, my mom and pa, my sisters and brothers, they'd all be shunned. I just can't let that happen."

Geoff felt like his guts were twisting. "What are you saying?"

Eli turned to face him. "I have to go back. For the sake of my family, I must go back." He covered his face with his hands as sobs racked his frame.

CHAPTER 16

GEOFF moved closer. There was no way he could sit by and not comfort Eli. Taking Eli in his arms, Geoff felt him move closer, resting his head on his shoulder as the sobs continued. "Are you sure you're not overreacting?"

Eli pulled away. "You don't understand!" he yelled through his sobs. "I love you more than anything, but I can't let my family suffer because of it!" His frustration faded away as quickly as it rose. "I've thought about this almost all day. I knew what I had to do as soon as I woke up this morning; I've just been trying to figure out how to tell you without shattering your heart as much as this is shattering mine."

The sobs returned, and this time Eli didn't hold back. He threw himself at Geoff, holding him, squeezing him as he sobbed through heaved breaths.

Geoff knew he could tell Eli that he'd do anything to get him to stay. He'd sell everything and move them across the country; he'd get down on his knees and beg him to stay with him if he thought it would help, but it wouldn't. He loved Eli, heart and soul deep, and part of what he loved was that Eli was the most caring, giving person he'd ever met. How could he ask him to be any less than himself to stay? He realized he couldn't. "You sweet, sweet man." Geoff ran his fingers through Eli's hair. "I love you so much."

Eli's sobs began to abate. "I'm caught, and there's no easy answer. If I stay, I'll have you, but my family will suffer, and I'd never be able to see them again. If I go, I'll be giving up the one person I love more than any other, but I'll condemn my family to possible shunning by the community."

"But they haven't done anything."

"That's the worst of it, isn't it? They'll be considered guilty by association and condemned regardless. Not officially, but others will treat them badly. Papa is respected, a community leader, but he'll be pushed aside, and the family will be forced to live on the fringes. People will avoid them on the street. They'll go somewhere else for their bread. They won't buy Papa's furniture or help him when he has a big order." Eli looked up into Geoff's eyes. "I don't see any other way out."

Geoff's heart was breaking. He knew he was going to lose Eli, the man he loved, but it hurt him more to see Eli in such agony. He had to let him go; there was no other choice. "When will you leave?"

Eli sniffled softly. "I should go right away and not drag out the hurt and pain."

"No! You can go in the morning. I want one more night with you, one last chance to hold you and be with you, one last chance to say good-bye. I need something to last me the rest of my life."

Eli stood up, trying to get hold of himself. "I need that too." Sniffling softly, Eli went upstairs, and then Geoff heard a bedroom door close. Geoff considered following him but thought better of it. He needed time to think... no, that was the last thing he needed to do. He had just a few hours with Eli, and he was going to make the very most of them.

Geoff climbed the stairs and knocked on Eli's door. "Eli, it's me." Slowly, the door opened to reveal red, puffy eyes. "Come here." Tentatively, Eli moved into his arms, and Geoff drew him close. He wasn't going to turn down anything that got Eli in his arms. "It'll be all right."

"How?"

"I don't know. I wish I did. Is there anything you need to do?"

Eli shook his head. "I don't have much to take back with me."

"Oh." Geoff leaned to Eli, kissing him. Geoff knew that each kiss could be their last, so he was determined to make each one count, and this was no exception. Eli melted into him, and he went with it, devouring those sensual lips and the sweet mouth before slowly pulling away. "I'll be right back up."

Geoff turned around and went downstairs, heading to the kitchen. He made a simple dinner, put the food on a tray, and after a stop in the living room, carried the tray up to the bedroom. He knocked, and Eli opened the door wearing the pink micro bikini.

Geoff's eyes bugged out. "What's this?"

"Raine left this for me, and I really wanted to wear it for you."

Geoff put the tray on the dresser and slipped off his shirt and pants, standing in front of Eli in only his underwear. "I brought us some dinner." He leaned forward. "Then it's just us."

Their kiss was almost enough to buckle Geoff's knees. He led Eli to the bed and made sure he was comfortable, brought over the tray, and joined him on the comforter. Geoff had confined dinner to finger foods. He picked up a bunch of grapes and fed them to Eli one at a time. Then Eli fed him the strawberries, with Geoff licking

Eli's fingers every chance he got. Tongue, hands, lips, it didn't matter how he touched Eli; he just knew he had to, like he needed to get a lifetime of touches in just a few hours.

Once they'd finished eating, Geoff put the tray back on the dresser, standing at the foot of the bed. Eli looked incredible in the pink bathing suit, the tight fabric leaving very little to the imagination. He wanted to remember, sear the image on his brain for later. Slowly, he climbed on the bed, crawling to where Eli waited for him. Gently, almost carefully, their lips touched, their tongues exploring.

They didn't hurry but let things build slowly. Eli moaned softly as Geoff shifted him down on the bed and lowered his body onto Eli's, their skin coming into contact. Using one hand, Geoff worked the fabric off Eli's body and then his own, pressing them together, his mind, the very cells of his skin crying out for as much contact with Eli as possible.

They made love for hours, Eli loving Geoff, and then Geoff loving Eli. Hands, lips, tongues, fingers… They caressed, tasted, gave, and took everything they wanted or needed. Hours they loved… soft and slow, fast and hard… it didn't matter. They needed each other, and they loved each other with everything they had. This was the last time, and they made the absolute most of it. Devouring one another, filling one another, memorizing every muscle, every contour, every taste and scent.

At almost midnight, completely sated and drained, they curled together on the bed, holding one another tightly, knowing this was the last time they'd get to do this.

"I have something for you." Geoff got out of bed and went to his dresser. "I want you to have this." He handed Eli a small photograph. "Len took this just after I returned to the farm."

Eli reached out and took the photo, a tear running down his face. "I don't have anything for you."

"I don't need anything." Geoff turned out the light and held Eli close, almost afraid to close his eyes for fear Eli would be gone when he opened them. Geoff told himself that he wasn't going to cry, wasn't going to break down while Eli was here. There would be plenty of time after he left to fall apart, and Geoff knew he would, but not until Eli was gone. At some point in the night, he did fall asleep, only to wake to the feel of the bed moving, but it was just Eli rolling over, and he closed his eyes again.

When Geoff next opened his eyes, the sun was just peeking through the windows. Eli was still asleep next to him, and Geoff was afraid to move. He knew that once Eli woke, it was the beginning of the end. So he breathed slowly and watched him. Those lips moving ever so slowly, eyelids fluttering occasionally, that smooth chest, milky white skin that felt so good beneath his hands, thick head of black hair. God, he'd never be able to look at Kirk with his shiny black coat and not think of Eli's rich, shiny hair.

That almost did it, almost made him cry, but he pushed it away and rested his head against the pillow. Geoff watched as Eli's blue eyes fluttered open, and Geoff kissed him softly. Eli moved closer, holding him tight and returning the kiss. Then he slowly got up. They both knew that the longer they dragged this out, the harder it was going to be.

"I'll meet you downstairs." Eli slipped out of the bed and quietly left the room.

After a while, Geoff got out of bed as well, pulling on a shirt and a pair of jeans. Without thinking, he went into the bathroom, brushing his teeth before stepping into a pair of shoes and heading downstairs. Eli was waiting for him, dressed in the clothes he'd worn when he arrived, looking once again like the proper Amish young man.

"Do you want me to drive you?"

Eli shook his head. "No, I'll walk."

Geoff nodded slowly but didn't move. He didn't know what to do. Finally, Eli stepped forward and hugged him, and then he tilted his head and kissed him gently before slowly turning away and walking out the front door. Geoff heard the dogs outside running to Eli for scratches. After a few minutes, he heard footsteps descend the porch stairs.

Geoff stood there, unmoving, for the longest time. His breathing was measured, like he'd stop if he didn't force his lungs to suck in the air. Slowly, he turned and forced his feet to lift as he climbed the stairs. At the landing, he saw that the door to Eli's room was open. Geoff knew that in his mind, it would always be Eli's room. He went inside.

On the bed were the jeans and shirts that Eli had worn while he was at the farm, along with the pink bathing suit and a note. With shaking hands, Geoff picked up the piece of paper.

My beloved Geoff,

I have nothing else to leave you, so I thought I would leave you this note. As I write this, you are still in bed in the other room, and I can still hear your soft breathing in my ear.

I wanted to take this chance to thank you, for taking me in, giving me a place to live, and most of all, for loving me the way you have. You taught me that I am worthy of being loved, and for that I will be eternally grateful. Wherever I go and whatever I do, I will think of you often. I will always remember you on Kirk, flying across the pasture like you're chasing the very wind itself, and the way you looked when we made love.

I will never forget you. No matter how long
I live or wherever life takes me, you will always be
there. I will never be able to ride a horse, see a
field of wildflowers, or pass a pasture of grazing
cattle without thinking of you and the love we
shared.

I will love you always,

Eli

Geoff dropped the paper and it fluttered to the floor when he saw that Eli had scrawled the words "Your Tiger" beneath his name.

Without thinking, Geoff walked to his bedroom and shut the door, leaning against it. Slowly, his knees gave out, and he slid down the door until he was resting on the floor. Covering his face with his hands, his feelings caught up to him, and he sobbed uncontrollably, his shoulders heaving with grief.

Eventually, tears wouldn't come anymore. Slowly, Geoff got to his feet and stood at the foot of the bed. Suddenly, in a moment of clarity, he realized the answer to the question he'd asked himself the day he'd first moved into this bedroom. He stared at the bed—the bed he and Eli had shared, the same bed his dad and Len had shared—and he knew. He knew what his dad and Len had done on their last night together. He hoped they'd made love one last time, but he knew they'd held each other close, and he knew that when the time came, Len had let his father go, the same way Geoff had let Eli go. He knew they'd talked to one another, told each other how much they loved each other, how much they meant to each other. He knew, too, that in the morning, they'd said good-bye to one another and kissed each other one last time. He could practically see Len getting out of bed and leaving the room, leaving the pills on the nightstand, doing what had to be done regardless of his own pain.

At the time, he'd asked himself how you'd thank someone for twenty years of love. He knew the answer to that too. Even though he'd only had Eli for two months, he knew. The answer was so simple.

You didn't have to.

"Geoff." He heard Len's voice calling from downstairs. Forcing his feet to move, he opened the door and made his way to the kitchen. "Would you tell Eli that breakfast is ready?"

Geoff shook his head, "Eli's gone."

"Gone... gone where?"

Geoff forced himself to say the words, hoping he wouldn't break down again, "He went back to the community. He's gone."

"God, Geoff, I'm so sorry." Len was right there, hugging him close, and Geoff tried not to start crying again, but he just couldn't help it. The tears came unbidden to his eyes, falling freely down his cheeks.

"Thanks, Len." He felt the arms slip away, and he sank into a chair, staring at the food in front of him. Slowly, he forced himself to eat something, but he wasn't hungry in the least. Giving up, he pushed back the chair and walked through the house and back up the stairs, his feet taking him directly to Eli's room.

Moving slowly but deliberately, he took the clothes stacked neatly on the bed and placed them back in the dresser. Picking up the letter from the floor, he folded it and tucked it into the drawer along with the clothes. Changing his mind, he took it out again. Leaving the room, he closed the door behind him and went to his own room. Opening the small drawer, he took out the envelope that held the letter from his dad and placed Eli's letter with it.

Ordinary farm noises filtered in through the window, reminding him that life went on regardless of his broken heart.

Forcing himself to move, Geoff put the envelope back in the drawer and went downstairs and outside, walking to the barn to start the day's chores. He got right to work, cleaning the few stalls that needed cleaning and keeping himself busy. It seemed to be working okay until he opened Kirk's stall and saw the shiny black stallion. Images of Eli flooded his mind, eyes dancing, black hair shining in the morning sun. He closed the stall door and quietly headed back to the house.

CHAPTER 17

GEOFF woke at his usual time and smiled to himself as he started to feel around the bed. Then he realized it was empty, and his smile faded. This had happened every morning for the last week. For those first few seconds, he forgot that Eli was gone. For those first few seconds, he felt happy. The rest of the day was just work. Even things that he used to find fun had turned to drudgery. He still rode every morning but got no joy out of it. He did it because the horses needed exercise, not because he wanted to.

Throwing back the covers, he got his butt out of bed, dressed, and went downstairs to the kitchen. Len was already there, and they talked about the day's activities while they had their coffee. "Joey asked if we had any work he could do. I think he really needs a summer job."

"Of course. Hire him on for the summer. We could use the help." With Eli gone, they were a man short, and they were going to have extra projects once they closed on the purchase of the Winters' farm.

Len smiled. "I thought you'd feel that way, so he'll be starting today."

Geoff shook his head. "Why didn't you just tell me you hired him? I trust your judgment. You are the foreman, after all." Geoff finished his coffee. "We should be on the lookout for another full-time hand. I think we're going to need the help, particularly once we expand the herd."

"I'll do that." Len finished his coffee while Geoff put his mug in the sink and headed to the barn.

For the first time in a week, he walked directly to Kirk's stall and began brushing and saddling the stallion. "You ready for a ride, boy?" The sable creature certainly seemed to be bouncing in his stall. Once he was done, Geoff led the horse outside and mounted. "Okay boy, let's go."

He spurred the horse on, and Kirk took off, running like the wind. They'd done it before, but this morning the speed and the wind began to clear away some of the cobwebs. He'd been fighting moving on, but now he realized he had to.

Kirk reached the other side of the pasture and slowed. Geoff turned him around and spurred him on again. Another race across the pasture did them both good. Then Geoff slowed Kirk to a walk, and they headed to one of the other pastures to check on the herd.

The long ride had done Geoff good, and after unsaddling his mount, he led Kirk into one of the paddocks and then headed inside, greeting Joey along the way. "Morning."

"Morning, Geoff." The teenager was smiling excitedly. "Thanks for the job. I promise I'll do my best."

"I know you will, Joey. What's Len got you starting on?"

"He says I need to keep the barn swept, the stalls clean, and the tack organized and ready for use." Joey's smile faded as he concentrated on what he'd be doing. "He also told me to keep track of our hay usage so we can make sure we put enough up for the winter."

"Excellent. And we'll probably need your help building fences in a few weeks." Geoff started toward the house but turned around. "Come to the house for lunch."

"Mom packed me a lunch." Joey held up a small brown bag.

"Okay, but you tell your mom that you're eating with the men from now on." That got him a huge smile. Joey was a good worker, and Geoff knew he'd pull his weight. Besides, it would be easier on his mom if she didn't need to worry about buying lunch things.

"I'll tell her." Joey waved as he headed in the barn to get to work.

Geoff's good mood lasted until he walked in the house and heard voices in the living room. *What's she doing here?* Walking in, he saw that he had a house full of relatives. His three aunts, Uncle Dan, and his cousins Jill and Chris, along with Len, were all sitting in the living room. "What are you all doing here?" He couldn't help glaring at his Aunt Janelle.

"We came to share some news." His Aunt Vicki was glowing, and he shifted his attention to his cousin, zeroing in on her hand. Pete had finally proposed.

"Well, I see congratulations are in order." Geoff hugged his cousin tightly. "You're a very lucky lady."

"Thank you." Jill was absolutely glowing.

"I have something for you. Just a minute." Geoff went upstairs to this room and grabbed a bundle from the closet before returning. "I want you to have this as a wedding present." Geoff heard his Aunt Janelle inhale sharply. "This was your great-grandmother's.

She and her mother made it for her wedding, and since you're the first one of our generation to marry, I think it should go to you."

She took the quilt with wide-eyed surprise and gently unfolded it. "Thank you, Geoff." She then hugged him and sat back down, admiring the gift.

His aunt Mari changed the subject. "Geoff, the real reason we're here is we've been worried about you. Since Eli left, you haven't been yourself." He didn't argue with her, but he had no intention of pretending to be happy either. Janelle humphed softly.

"I'm fine. I'll get past it eventually, but it'll take time." He truly doubted he'd get over it any time soon, but he didn't want her to feel bad.

"If you ask me, you're better off without him. Now you can find a nice girl and get married." Janelle's sanctimonious tone grated up Geoff's spine like nails on a blackboard.

His temper flared, and he turned on her, giving her his full attention. "First thing you better get through your thick head is that I'm gay. I will never meet a girl, settle down, and get married. That just isn't going to happen."

Geoff's anger was starting to get the better of him. He'd been holding it in for a week, and it wouldn't be held in any longer. "And don't think I don't know that you're the one spreading rumors around town."

"I speak my mind!"

"Spread lies is more like it. Lies that got us *attacked* a week ago." Geoff heard gasps but kept going. "Lies that hurt the one person who means more to me than anyone else in this world. Someone so kind and caring that he left because *your* lies would hurt his family!"

Geoff wiped his eyes and kept going. "And they hurt me. A member of my own family deliberately spread rumors to hurt me. Well, I hope you're happy because it worked. He's gone, and I'm miserable without him." Geoff turned and started to walk away. "I want you gone."

"What?" That sanctimonious tone was back, and Geoff snapped.

"I want you gone!" He pointed at her. "You have five minutes, you hurtful, spiteful bitch, to get off my property, or I'll have you arrested for trespassing!" He pointed to the door. "Get out!"

Janelle stood up. "Come, Victoria, we're leaving." She started to walk to the door.

"I'm not going anywhere. He's my nephew, and he's right. You are a spiteful bitch, and I'm tired of you."

Janelle looked like a fish caught on a lure, her mouth hung so far open. "Then how am I going to get home?"

"We'll take you home when we're ready." Vicki looked like she was just getting comfortable.

Geoff looked at his watch and relented. "You can stay until they're ready to leave. But I don't want to see you or hear you. Go sit on the porch. Maybe the dogs will keep you company, if they're feeling charitable. And after today, I never want to speak to you or hear from you again."

Geoff's anger had run its course and began dying away. "Excuse me." Geoff turned and left the room, sitting at the kitchen table.

A few minutes later, Mari and Vicki sat down across from him. "I'm not going to apologize to her, so don't ask. I'm hurting right now, and she's partially responsible," Geoff said.

"You'll get over this and find someone else. This isn't the end of the world."

He knew Aunt Vicki meant well. "It sure feels like it." He looked up at them. "I spent a lot of time in Chicago with a lot of men. Hell, I had sex with three or four different men a week sometimes, but nothing compared to what I feel for him." They didn't understand so he tried again.

"Do you believe in having a soul mate, someone who completes you in a way you never thought possible?" They both nodded. "Well, Eli was mine—I know that. I can feel it with every fiber of my being, and now he's gone. He's less than ten miles away, and he might as well be on the other side of the world. Hell… he *is* in another world, a completely different world."

Vicki took his hand. "Honey, he chose to go back. You have to see that."

"I know he did. He chose to go back because her rumors threatened to hurt his family. If word got back to them that he was gay, his entire family would be shunned. Don't you understand? He gave up his own happiness for his family."

Two sets of eyes looked at him, definitely confused. "He's gay. By leaving he's condemned himself to live a lie for the rest of his life. He'll probably marry and have children, but his wife will never make him happy, no matter how hard she tries, and she won't know why, and he'll never be able to tell her. I know I'm unhappy, but he's the one who'll be unhappy for the rest of his life." The looks on his aunts' faces told him they were at least starting to understand.

"My God, he's in a prison." Mari put her hand over her mouth.

"And it's a life sentence." Geoff didn't try to keep the pain out of his voice. He had a pretty good idea of how hard Eli was going to have it for the rest of his life.

"What can we do?"

"Nothing. The only person who can do anything is Eli, and he's made his decision. It hurts, but his caring nature is part of why I love him. I can't expect him to care about his family any less than he cares about me." It was true. He'd never have forced Eli to choose between him and his family.

"You need to move on." Geoff shook his head—Vicki just didn't understand. But she was trying, and he had to give her credit for that. "Aunt Vicki, if Eli was a woman, would you be telling me the same thing?"

Geoff could almost see the light go on behind his aunt's eyes, "Oh goodness. I'd... we'd be supportive and let you grieve for the loss." Before Geoff could nod, she was on her feet, rushing to his side of the table, hugging him tight. "You take as much time as you need. We'll be here for you. We're just worried about you."

"I know, and I appreciate it." Geoff hugged her back and then got up. "Did you want to go for a ride?"

"Not today." She looked toward the front of the house, "I should take Janelle home before she explodes."

"I meant what I said." He looked at both his aunts. "I never want to have anything to do with her again. There's enough hate and bigotry in the world. I don't need it from my family, and I won't have it in my house."

"You know she'll be at Jill's wedding."

The last thing he wanted was to put his family in a difficult position. "Just don't put us at the same table, and we'll be fine." Geoff winked, and they both hugged him again before rejoining the rest of the family in the living room.

189

"Dan, we should get going. Geoff's got things to do." They all got up, and after exchanging hugs and saying their good-byes, they left. The house was quiet again with only Len sitting in his chair.

"I went to the bakery this morning. I saw Eli while I was there."

Geoff felt hope flare inside him and then die back down. "How is he?"

"I didn't get a chance to talk to him—his uncle was there. But he smiled. His uncle recognized me from when I brought Eli to visit. He told me Eli was doing well and that he was acclimating well and planned to join the community next week." Len looked at Geoff, a little puzzled. "That was exactly what he said, but I don't know what it means."

Geoff felt his legs wobble, and he flopped on the sofa to keep from falling. That was it, after next week…. "It means that next week, Eli is scheduled to be baptized into the church. That he'll take his place as an adult member of the Amish community."

He'd known this was coming, but just hearing about it was a little overwhelming. Geoff felt the last bit of hope he'd been clinging to slip from his grip.

Every day, he'd hoped that Eli would somehow return to him, that he'd change his mind and come back. Now he realized how ridiculous he was being. He had to move on. Somehow, he had to figure out how he was going to live the rest of his life without Eli.

Geoff got to his feet and went into the office, shutting the door quietly. He'd just sat at the desk when he heard a soft knock. "It's open."

Len cracked the door and stepped inside. "Up 'til now, I haven't been able to bring myself to come in here. It reminded me too much of Cliff." Len stood in front of the desk, just looking around. "I can still see him sitting at that desk, working, planning, smoking one of his damned cigars near the window so I wouldn't find out."

Len's voice sounded so careful. "I had Cliff for twenty years, and I enjoyed every minute I had with him. I know you had Eli for just a few months, but it doesn't make the loss any less overpowering or any less meaningful." Len sat down as Geoff watched the man he considered a father share some of his own grief.

"I can tell you that it gets better. I still miss him, and I probably always will. Each morning when I wake up, I forget he's gone for about thirty seconds, then I remember."

Geoff looked into those eyes that had watched him ride his first horse, watched his baseball games, and watched over him when he was sick, and realized just how lucky he was. Getting up from his chair, he walked to Len and hugged him. "I love you, Dad."

"Dad?"

"Yeah, I think it's time I stopped calling you Len. You're my father, as much as he was, so I'm going to call you Dad." Geoff watched as Len wiped his eyes. "I'm one of the lucky ones; I've got two."

The two men hugged each other for a while, both of them sniffling softly as they shared their loss.

Then Len pulled away and wiped his eyes for a final time. "I think we both need to stop, or we'll start screaming hysterically like Sally Field. 'I wanna know why?'" Both Geoff and Len started to laugh at Len's near perfect imitation. When they'd gotten control of themselves again, they went to work, and Geoff had to admit he felt better.

CHAPTER 18

GEOFF and Kirk flew across the pasture, the speed and the feeling of being one with the horse clearing out the morning cobwebs. He didn't let himself reminisce about how much he missed his morning rides with Eli. He couldn't. Pushing his hurt aside was the only way he could get through the day. The nights... oh, the nights were another matter all together.

Geoff reined in his horse and yawned. He hadn't been sleeping very well. Every night, as soon as he fell asleep, he'd dream of Eli and wake up incredibly disappointed. Two nights ago, he'd dreamed that Eli had come back. The details of his dream had been so vivid, so realistic, that when he woke and Eli wasn't there, it felt like he'd lost him all over again.

"Sorry, boy. I guess I haven't been good company lately." The horse's head bobbed as though he was agreeing with him. Geoff patted Kirk's neck, "You didn't have to agree with me; you could have lied." Kirk chose that moment to turn his head to look at him with one of those huge brown eyes. "Okay, okay, let's head back." Geoff turned them around and urged Kirk into a trot. "Jesus, I'm carrying on a conversation with a horse." Geoff smirked as they trotted back toward the barn.

In the yard, he dismounted and walked the horse into his stall. After unsaddling, he turned him out into his paddock. Outside, he stopped and watched the colt running and frolicking as his mother stood watching. Princess ambled over to Geoff, and he fed her a few carrots and petted her nose.

With a sigh, he turned and walked to the house, seeing his Aunt Mari's car parked in the drive. Out of habit, he checked his watch. Something must be wrong—it wasn't even eight. Aunt Mari may have grown up on a farm, but she was rarely up before nine on a weekend.

The door slammed behind him as he walked into the kitchen, "What brings you here so ear—?" Geoff stopped short as Eli's blue eyes looked back at him.

His aunt smiled. "I picked up a hitchhiker as I was going into town." Geoff heard her voice, but his vision narrowed to only Eli. Mari and Len stood up, and Geoff was vaguely aware of them leaving the room.

Geoff's heart leapt, but he tamped it down. "Are you just visiting or here to stay?" Having Eli return definitely fit in the too-good-to-be-true category.

Eli's eyes showed insecurity and worry. "If you'll have me. I mean, I'd like to stay, but if you don't want me that way, I'll understand. But if nothing else, I need a job."

"If I'll have you?" Geoff's feet moved with a mind of their own. "*If I'll have you?*" Then he was right there, pulling Eli into his arms, holding him tight. "I'm never letting you go again." Geoff's lips crashed onto Eli's, holding him tight, his hand carding through dark hair, increasing the pressure on their lips.

"Geoff, I'm...." Mari's voice trailed off, but Geoff barely heard her and didn't stop their kissing. His entire being was glued to Eli, the feel of his body next to his, the soft silky hair against his fingers. The taste of his lips, the scent of his skin, the small moans all combined to fill his senses, and right now there was no room for anything else. The house could burn down around them, and Geoff would hardly notice. Eli was there in his arms, kissing him, holding him tight, and that was all that mattered.

The sharp sound of the back screen door closing brought him back to the here and now, and he slowly pulled back from the kiss, looking into Eli's eyes. "Are you really back? This isn't some trick or something? I'm not imagining this?"

"No, no trick. And it's not your imagination." Eli's eyes clouded. "I'm here for as long as you'll have me." There was a touch of nervousness in his voice. Geoff just held him, reveling in the feel of having Eli back in his arms.

Len breezed into the kitchen. "I'm headed out to get the guys started on those fences." Geoff nodded and looked up from Eli's shoulder, not ready to let him go. "Are you going to stay?" Len asked.

"Yes."

"Good." Len put his mug in the sink. "Don't hurt him again."

"I won't if I can help it." Len glared at Eli, and then a small smile crept onto his face before he left the kitchen, the screen door slamming behind him.

Geoff was torn between pulling Eli upstairs and tearing his clothes off and finding out what happened and why Eli was here. The sound of the men in the yard helped him decide, and he released Eli and directed him toward the living room.

"I never expected to see you again. Not that I'm complaining, but what happened?" Geoff sat on the sofa and tugged Eli down next to him.

"I was miserable the entire time I was gone. Whenever I wasn't busy, I'd think of you. So I worked the entire time." Eli leaned against Geoff, needing to feel his lover as much as Geoff needed to feel him. "When I got home, everyone was happy and welcomed me back. Initially, things were good. I was back among people I knew, and everything was familiar. But you weren't there." Eli stopped and wiped his eyes. "I can't tell you how many times I turned to tell you something before realizing you weren't there. A few times I actually said your name. Luckily Papa didn't hear me."

Eli stopped and took a deep breath. "Papa was so happy I returned. He put me to work with him, helping him in the shop, and scheduled my baptism in the church. In his mind, I was back with the family and everything was perfect."

Geoff nodded slowly. "Len said your uncle told him that you were becoming an adult member of the community. When he told me, that was when I gave up hope of seeing you again. Until then I'd kept looking, thinking maybe you'd change your mind and come back to me. But after that, I stopped letting myself hope."

"I'm sorry."

Geoff shook his head, not able to say anything, so he let his kiss speak for him. Eli went with it, letting Geoff press him back against the sofa cushions. Geoff could barely think. Eli was here, that's all that mattered. Explanations could wait, talking could wait; his body and mind were screaming for Eli. He needed to touch him, feel him. Geoff forced himself to get up from the sofa and tugged Eli to his feet, practically dragging him up the stairs and down the hall to the bedroom.

He hooked the door with his foot, closing it with a bang. The noise hardly registered as he advanced on Eli like a cat stalking its prey. Geoff worked the buttons on his shirt, opening it, slipping it off his shoulders before dropping it to the floor. His eyes never wavered from Eli as he moved forward. He saw Eli back up until his legs bumped the bed, but Geoff kept prowling closer. His fingers opened his belt, pulling it off, dropping it with a clunk. Shoes thumped as they bounced after flipping from his feet. His pants opened almost on their own, denim fabric kicked off, another addition to the trail on the floor.

Eli hadn't moved, his eyes following every movement, and Geoff swore he could see his own passion mirrored in those eyes. Geoff reached his prey, taking the hat Eli still carried and tossing it away before grabbing Eli's shirt and using it to pull him forward. Their lips crashed together, need and passion swamping Geoff's already lust-clouded mind. His hands pulled, and buttons pinged to the floor as they popped off the shirt. Fabric tore as he pulled the shirt off his lover's body before crushing their chests together. Only then did his feral yearning begin to subside into needy passion.

His hands devoured the skin on Eli's back, gripping and palming as much as he could. His chest heaved as they moved together. Eli's nipples, pointy and hard, rubbed against his chest. "Yes!" Geoff groaned. That was just what he needed. "Get those pants off if you want them in one piece." Geoff watched as the belt was opened and Eli's pants fell to the floor, and then Geoff pushed him back on the bed. He pulled off his lover's shoes and yanked off his pants before tossing them over his shoulder.

He watched Eli's eyes as he crawled on the bed, his hands sliding up his legs and chest. "I dreamed about this for the past two weeks, that you'd come back to me. Every morning when I woke up I wondered where you were, why you weren't in my bed." Geoff settled across Eli's waist, pinning him to the mattress. "Every morning, I was happy for a moment until I remembered you weren't here." Geoff took one of Eli's wrists in each hand, holding them over his head. "I missed you like I'd miss my hand or foot. Without you I was incomplete." Then he leaned forward, kissing the man splayed out beneath him.

Eli vibrated against him. "I missed you too. Every time I smelled hay or rode one of the horses, I thought of you. When Len came in the bakery, it took all my willpower not to rush to him. When he left, I had to stop myself from yelling for him to take me with him." Eli's eyes glistened with tears.

The tears in Eli's eyes cooled Geoff's ardor just enough, and he released his wrists before pulling Eli close, holding his lover tight. "Never going to let you go again. I didn't fight this time, but I will next time, with everything I have." Geoff brought their lips together again. This time, the kiss was less bruising, less possessive, and much more loving. His hands slid over Eli's chest, letting that hot skin slide beneath his palms. His hands remembered the feel of that skin, the contours of Eli's chest.

Eli moaned softly into Geoff's mouth as a hand slid down his stomach and beneath the band of his underwear. Geoff's fingers circled around the hard, silky shaft beneath the fabric. "Geoff," Eli whined softly as he bucked into his hand. "No one ever touches me like you."

"I sincerely hope not." Geoff pumped his hand slowly, feeling Eli stiffen even more in his hand.

Eli smiled into Geoff's lips. "You know what I mean."

Geoff did know, but he liked hearing it just the same. Moving his fingers, Geoff slid the fabric down Eli's hips so Eli could work them off. Then he slid his own underwear down, kicking them aside. Eli's body, his erection rubbing against his, felt like coming home. This was what he'd missed so much: the closeness, the loving. He could almost feel his heart sighing in relief now that the rest of him had come back.

Geoff let his lips travel, relearning the scent and taste of his lover: the feel and taste of those perky nipples, the flat belly, the heady musk as he approached Eli's sex. He slid his tongue down the hard length, swirling around the head as Eli's special flavor burst in his mouth. He wanted more, needed more. Opening wide, he took Eli deep in one motion.

"God, Geoff!"

Geoff smiled as he bobbed his head slowly, sliding his lips around Eli's length, listening to the steady stream of soft, beautiful music Eli was making. It thrilled him beyond measure that Eli was making those sounds for him. No one else had ever heard Eli make those sounds—only Geoff. Eli's music was becoming more urgent, and he backed away, letting his lover breathe. "Not yet, Tiger. Gonna make you wait."

He got a small whine, and then Eli was flipping them on the bed, his Tiger taking what he wanted. Eli's weight now pressed Geoff against the mattress, but this wasn't what he wanted, not right now.

"Sit up, Tiger."

Eli shifted, straddling Geoff's hips. Geoff placed his hands beneath Eli's butt and lifted, scooting him forward until he sat on his chest. Geoff guided Eli to lie back, pulling his hips forward. Craning his neck up, he licked around Eli's opening. That music started again almost immediately, and Eli scooted closer. Geoff teased the puckered skin with his fingers while his tongue probed and sucked.

"Missed this so much. Missed you the entire time," Eli moaned.

"I know, Tiger. Gonna make up for lost time." Eli's skin puckered and throbbed as he blew on it, moans drifting up from where Eli lay all spread out on top of him. Letting one hand roam, he stroked Eli's stomach while the other drove Eli wild with desire.

"Want you, Geoff. Can't take much more." That was becoming very plain. Eli was throbbing on top of him, his body shaking as he moaned and whimpered.

"Okay, Tiger." Geoff wet a finger and slid it deep into Eli, that hot body pulling him in, his finger nearly burning from the heat.

Eli wriggled on Geoff's finger, wanting more, so Geoff added a second, and Eli pushed against it, sucking it right in. "Geoff, need you so bad. Need it to be you."

"Will be in a second. Need to make sure you're ready." Eli pulled off Geoff's fingers and sat up, spitting on his hand. Wetting Geoff's dripping erection, he positioned himself and took him in, driving down in a single long motion.

"Yes!" Eli cried out when he rested against his lover's hips.

Geoff thought his head was going to explode. Every nerve in his body seemed to be firing at the same damn time. Hell, it was so hot when his Tiger took what he wanted.

Geoff started to move, but Eli stilled his hips with a touch. "I'm the Tiger." He lifted his body and slammed back down onto Geoff.

"Elijah—" Geoff could barely breathe, and he gasped for air, catching his breath just as Eli repeated the motion, stealing his breath away again. "Tiger—"

"That's right." Eli lifted his body again. "I'm the Tiger, so I'm in charge." Then he slammed back down. "I love you, Geoff, and you're mine!" This time he gripped Geoff as tight as he could and fucked himself on his lover like the hounds of hell were after them. Geoff tried to form words, make sounds, anything, but all he could do was hang on and let Eli do the driving.

He could feel the pressure building deep inside him. Reaching up, he began to stroke hard along Eli's length. "Come for me, Tiger.

Want you to come on my cock." Eli's eyes scrunched shut, and his rhythm became erratic. Crying out, he shot on Geoff's stomach.. The throbbing pressure and clenching muscles drove Geoff to his own release, and he came deeply in his lover as lights danced behind his eyes.

Slowly, Eli lifted himself off Geoff, both of them whimpering when Geoff slipped out. After a quick cleanup, they scooted together, arms curled around each other, their immediate need sated.

"I thought I'd lost you forever. What made you come back?" Geoff asked.

Eli rested his head on Geoff's shoulder, fingers tracing circles on his lover's chest. "My mom, actually."

Geoff turned his head to look into Eli's eyes. He couldn't believe Eli was serious.

"She took me aside yesterday and told me that she could see I wasn't happy. She asked me if I'd met someone when I was away, and there was no way I could outright lie to her, so I told her yes."

"Then why'd you come back?" His mother had said as she worked on her sewing.

Eli had hung his head, not able to explain fully. "The English world is harsh and cruel."

She continued her work as she spoke. "I know it can be cruel, but you found love, and that's too precious to turn your back on." She stilled her hands and put down her sewing. "You're not happy, and while I don't want you to go, I want what every mother wants, to see her children as happy as possible." She looked around the room to make sure no one could hear, "You need to go back. Once you take your vows and receive baptism, you'll be trapped for the rest of your life." Eli had tried to argue with her, but she'd quieted him. "My oldest brother was just like you." She'd smiled as she remembered. "He left for a year away, just like you, but came back and hid his true self. He rejoined the community, got baptized, and married. He was miserable for the rest of his life. Your papa thinks it's because he had the devil in him." She'd shaken her head softly. "Far be it from me to argue with your Papa, but I know it was because he found happiness outside and turned his back on it. He regretted what he'd done till the day he died." She wiped a tear from her eye.

"What do I do?"

"Be honest with your Papa like you always have. Tell him what you're feeling, and in the morning you'll leave. He may be angry for a while, but he'll get over it." Eli's mother swallowed hard. "After tomorrow it's too late."

Geoff scooted closer, holding his sweet lover close. "What did he say when you told him?"

"Not much. He looked disappointed, but he actually seemed to understand. Mama may have spoken to him first. I don't really know. He did say that he wanted me to be sure to visit, so I think it will be okay."

"I know you can never tell them about us." It made Geoff sad that Eli was going to have to hide who he was from his family. "But what if someone finds out?"

"We'll worry about that when the time comes, if it ever does. Mama made me realize that I have to be true to them as well as myself. And being true to myself means being here with you. Besides, as time passes, I'll fade from the community. They'll move ahead without me."

Geoff turned his head, kissing his lover tenderly. "Not only are you the kindest, sweetest, most giving person I've ever met, you're the bravest too."

"No, I'm not."

"Yes, you are. It takes a brave person to give up everything for love." Eli'd given up his family and the only life he'd ever known for him. Geoff just hoped he could live up to that.

"I didn't give up anything." Eli rolled onto his side. "Instead, I have everything, because I have you."

Geoff faced his lover. "Then we're both lucky, because we have each other." Geoff leaned in for another kiss and pulled Eli to him, his body responding immediately.

Eli stopped him gently. "I have to get to work. Don't want the boss unhappy."

"I know him; he can be a real pain in the butt."

Eli got off the bed, walking gingerly. "Don't I know it." Geoff tried to swat the butt in question, but Eli dodged away, laughing as he began picking up his clothes. Eli held up his shirt. "Don't think I can wear this again."

"I put your clothes in the dresser in your old room." Geoff pulled on his pants and began buttoning his shirt.

"Old room. You don't want me to stay here? But I thought—"

"Eli, I want you to stay here in this room, with me. When I asked you if you were staying, I meant with me, here in this room, sharing this bed, forever."

Eli broke into a smile and jumped into Geoff's arms. "Yes! Yes! Yes!" They began kissing again, and despite their earlier efforts, their clothes ended up scattered back on the floor. Chores could wait, the world could wait—right now, right here, it was just them.

EPILOGUE

GEOFF woke early, really early. He had things to do, and he didn't want Eli to know. Gingerly getting out of bed, he slipped out of the bedroom and into the bathroom, where he'd hidden his clothes. Somehow he managed to dress in the dark without killing himself. Opening the door slowly, he tiptoed through the room and out the bedroom door. Carefully walking down the stairs, he slipped into his insulated pants, boots, coat, gloves, and hat. Dressed like an Eskimo, he quietly headed outside through the fresh snow to the barn.

Geoff went right to the tack room and dug out part of Eli's Christmas present, putting it near the door so he'd remember to take it back inside. Then he made his way to each stall, filling mangers with hay and checking water buckets. Long, regal heads poked out of every stall. For years the lower portion of the barn had been bigger than they needed. The farm just didn't need twenty horses. But since Eli returned and began teaching riding with Len's help and blessing, he and Geoff had decided to fill fourteen of the stalls with boarders for Eli's riding students. They'd advertised briefly, but word had quickly spread in horse circles, and Eli earned a reputation as an excellent riding teacher. After two months, his classes were full, and he had a waiting list of students.

As he worked, Geoff began to get warm, so he pulled off his coat. Within an hour, all the horses were fed and watered. He checked on each horse, giving each a treat and making sure they were okay. Then he made sure the two steers were fed and watered. Joey had faithfully taken care of his two charges, and they were growing nicely. Geoff had specifically told Joey not to come to the barn today. His last stop was the stall of the colt. He was stunning, and soon there'd be two more. The colt's mother and Twilight were both expecting Kirk's foals, and Geoff was hoping one of them would have the stallion's rich, black coloring. He made sure all the doors were secure before heading back to the house with his surprise.

As he walked through the snow, he stopped in the middle of the yard, taking a minute to look around. The last several months had been both happy and sad. Losing his father had been hard, but he would never have found Eli without his father's passing. It was definitely a bittersweet thought. The purchase of the Winters' farm had gone off without a hitch. Frank had already planned all of the acreage for the next year, and they were making plans for future years. He'd even taken to puttering around the barn, helping with repairs. There was also the possibility of purchasing some additional hayfields, but that was for the future. Geoff couldn't stop himself from looking all around him. The farm was profitable, and much of the money he'd used to buy land had been replaced. Life was indeed good.

Geoff began to feel the cold starting to seep through his clothes, so he headed toward the house, filling his arms with firewood before opening the back door.

The house was still quiet as he put the wood near the stove and began peeling off his winter gear. Opening the back cupboard in the laundry room, he pulled out the rest of the presents, placing them under the tree. With a sneaky smile, he went back upstairs, undressed, and crawled back into bed.

Eli curled up to him and then jerked away. "Geez, where have you been? I'm not cuddling up to an ice cube."

"This ice cube just fed and watered all the horses so you don't have to get out of bed."

Eli gingerly kissed Geoff. "Thank you, but don't put your cold parts on me." Eli shifted away again, nearly falling off the mattress as Geoff started rubbing his butt. "No fair, you're too cold."

Geoff slunk away. "That's not cold." He reached over and pulled Eli to him. "This is cold." Eli shivered and tried to get away, but Geoff held him close.

"You're nice and warm."

Eli slapped him playfully. "And you're mean." Then he settled next to Geoff, finally cuddling close as he warmed up. "Just don't put your feet on me."

"I love you too much for that." Geoff's feet were like ice, even to him. "Merry Christmas, Tiger." He nuzzled Eli's neck, sucking gently on the warm skin.

"Merry Christmas." Eli rolled over, pressing close to Geoff. "Love you." Eli leaned close, nibbling on Geoff's ear. "Is it time for presents?" Before Geoff could react, Eli was out of bed running for the bathroom, laughing like a kid the entire way.

Shaking his head, Geoff got out of bed and pulled on some sweats and socks before going downstairs. Eli had gone a little nuts with the Christmas decorations. There were pine boughs strung everywhere. The house smelled like a forest. Eli had never had a Christmas tree before, so Len had taken him along when he looked for one to cut. Len said Eli had insisted on this tree—the top of it touched the ceiling. Geoff plugged in the lights on the tree and stood back. Eli had insisted on using only homemade ornaments, and they'd spent a lot of evenings making paper stars, painting wooden cutouts, and stringing popcorn and cranberries. Geoff turned around and saw Eli coming down the stairs.

"I thought you were crazy, but this is the best Christmas tree I've ever seen." It was stunning, covered in the ornaments they'd made together.

Eli moved into his arms. "Who's coming for dinner?"

"My Aunt Mari, Aunt Vicki and the family, along with Frank and Penny Winters."

"Maybe I should ask the really important question—who's cooking all the food? And don't you dare say you are."

Geoff laughed. "Aunt Mari and Aunt Vicki are actually doing the cooking. Well, most of it other than all the stuff you've baked for the last three days." Eli had filled the house with the scent of enough baking cookies, fresh bread, candy, and sweets to delight even Scrooge. "You've really made this Christmas special in so many ways. I know it's been hard for you being away from your family."

"You're my family, and it has been special, very special." They leaned together, kissing softly in the glow of the twinkling lights on the tree.

"You're so beautiful and handsome. I love you so much." Geoff tilted Eli's head gently and kissed him again, their bodies pressed together on their own, each finding the other. Geoff was tempted—how wonderful would it be to make love right here under the tree? But Len would be down soon. "Do you want your big present now or later?"

"What did you do?" Eli watched Geoff shrug and smirk. "I'll wait 'til later."

Geoff put another log in the stove and went to the kitchen, brewing coffee and starting a light breakfast. As he expected, the scent brought Len downstairs, yawning. "What is it with you two? It's a day off, and you're still up with the cows." Len yawned again. "You're worse now than you were as a kid."

"It's Christmas!" Geoff and Eli replied, and they laughed. Len's only reply was to shake his head and pad into the kitchen, returning with a steaming mug.

Len sat in his chair while Eli and Geoff went to the tree and started handing out presents. Eli went first, handing Geoff a wrapped box. Geoff opened it and gasped. Inside was a beautiful wooden desk set Eli had obviously made himself. "Thank you." Geoff pulled Eli to him for a hug.

"I thought you could use it when you do the accounts."

Geoff handed Eli the package he'd brought in from the barn that morning. "This is for you from both Dad and I." Geoff looked at Len and smiled.

Eli opened the package and looked at both of them, confused. "I'm sorry, I don't understand."

Geoff explained. "That's one of the name tags we use on the stalls."

"I see that, but why does it say Tiger on it?"

Geoff leaned real close. "I know I call you Tiger, but what else on this farm has that name?"

Eli's eyes went wide. "You're giving me the colt?" Eli sat on the floor, a tear rolling down that beautiful face.

"Merry Christmas."

Eli jumped up and gave Len a huge hug before throwing himself into Geoff's arms, hugging him tightly. "Thank you."

"You're welcome, Love."

Len got up and finished making breakfast, with Geoff and Eli joining him a few minutes later.

AFTER all the festivities, the huge dinner, and the house full of relatives, the late afternoon quiet was wonderfully refreshing. "Thank you for a wonderful Christmas," Eli said, looking at the glowing Christmas tree. "Where did Len say he was going?"

"To Chris's for a few hours."

Eli moved closer. "How do you feel about him dating?"

"I'm thrilled for him, actually. He went through a lot with Dad's cancer, and if he's ready to date again, then I'm happy. Besides, Chris is a great guy and really seems to like him. To tell you the truth, I'm just so in love, I want the world to be in love." Geoff had hired Chris toward the end of summer. He and Len had gotten along great from the start but had only started dating about a month ago. "Dad says that they're taking it slow."

Eli snuggled close. "That's what he says, but I see how he lights up whenever they're together." Eli smiled up at Geoff. Oh, he knew that lit-up look well. He'd seen Eli light up often enough over the last few months.

"Look." Geoff pointed out the window. Light snow had just started to fall in the fading twilight. "It's so beautiful." They stood together watching the snow, holding each other, but soon progressed to hot, slow, kissing. "I've got one more present for you, but this one's different. It's something we can work on together." Eli's eyes locked on Geoff's. "Frank has an old carriage in his garage. It'll need some work, but I thought we could do it together. We'd have to train one of the horses to pull it, but I thought it would be a fun project for us."

Eli's eyes widened. "Is it plain?"

Geoff shook his head. "It's really fancy, black with gold scrollwork and red upholstery. It'll be some work, but I thought we could take it to the fair next year if we get it done."

"You take such good care of me." Eli moved closer, as if that were possible. "Yes, I'd love to work on the carriage with you. When can I see it?" Eli's eyes were bright with excitement.

"We'll take the truck tomorrow and bring it back." The light outside was fading, the room getting darker, with only the tree for light.

Eli led him to the sofa, and when Geoff sat, Eli straddled his legs, pushing him back against the cushions before taking his lips in a smoldering kiss. "Love you."

Geoff's head lolled back against the cushions as Eli's hands pulled at the hem of his sweatshirt, pulling it up and off. "Love you too, Tiger. More than anything or anyone." He could feel a shudder travel through Eli. "When you were gone, I shut down, stopped feeling, stopped thinking—wanted only you."

Eli stood up, pulling off his shirt and slipping his pants down his legs. Without speaking, he tapped Geoff's hip. Geoff lifted up, and Eli tugged away the sweatpants. Then Eli was back, straddling his hips, that hot, hard cock rubbing against his stomach. Eli's lips kissed him hard, demanding, taking. "Never want to be without you again." Eli's hands roamed over Geoff's chest. "I need you, like I need to breathe."

Geoff's hands caressed Eli's shoulders, sliding down his back before cupping the firm butt. Their kisses became more urgent and needy. Hands became greedy, needing to touch. Geoff pulled Eli to him, pressing their chests together. Eli whimpered softly as Geoff's hand slid beneath him, fingers sliding across his opening. "Geoff, your hands; need more." Bringing a hand to Eli's lips, he slipped two fingers into his mouth. Eli sucked them deep, swirling his tongue around the digits. Then Geoff slipped his fingers from Eli's lips before pressing them to his lover's opening, swirling one against the muscle. Eli whined softly as Geoff's finger pressed into him, first to one knuckle and then two.

"You like that, Tiger?" Geoff sure did. Every time he moved his finger Eli rocked against him, that hot body and throbbing length brushing against him.

"Yeah, do that thing you do." Eli threw his head back, holding on to Geoff's shoulders.

Geoff added another finger, scissoring them inside his lover as he brushed against the spot that made Eli moan and vibrate against him. "Is that what you want?" Eli nodded as his eyes closed. "How about this?" Geoff twisted his fingers deep, and he felt Eli shudder against him, hot skin vibrating against his.

"Geoff, I need you soon." Eli's arms wound around his neck, holding on tight as Geoff continued playing Eli's body like a fine instrument.

"I know, Love." Slowly, Geoff removed his fingers and leaned to the floor next to the sofa to grab the lube. After slicking himself, he slowly slid into his lover. Eli's face glowed as he pushed inside, joining them together. "You're so beautiful like this. Love how you feel around me." Geoff flexed his hips, driving deep.

Eli threw his head back, crying out as Geoff filled him before pulling out and driving deep again. Geoff set a nice rhythm, and Eli met each movement, every stroke. Their lips came together, heating their passion. "Geoff… Love you."

"Love you too, Tiger." Eli surprised him by driving down onto Geoff, taking him deep and then lifting off again. "Not gonna last if you keep doing that." Eli just smiled and kept right on driving Geoff into him. "Stroke yourself, Tiger; want you to come with me."

Eli began to move, his hand sliding along his length. Geoff watched as his eyes rolled back, his face a mask of pure pleasure. "That's it, Love, give it to me. Show me how good it is." Eli's eyes popped open, and his head tilted back as he cried out softly. Geoff felt his lover's hot release paint his stomach. The contractions and the heat were too much. Geoff felt his own release barrel through him, and he poured himself deep in his lover.

Then he was being held close, lips moving against his, soft kisses soothing him out of his post-orgasmic haze.

"Love you, love you so much," Eli whispered as he was kissing him, and his hands petted Geoff's head as he slowly came down from one of the most intense orgasms of his life. Each time with Eli seemed better than the last, and this was no exception. Eli lifted himself off Geoff's legs and went to the kitchen, returning with paper towels and carefully wiped them clean. Geoff reclined on the sofa, and Eli nestled against him. Geoff covered them with the blanket, and he held Eli close, his chest pressed to Eli's back. The light outside continued to fade as they cuddled together.

"You always say that I'm beautiful. Will you still love me when I'm old?"

Geoff's hand made small circles on his stomach. "Elijah." Geoff rarely called him that, and he turned his head to look into Geoff's eyes. "I don't love you because you're beautiful. You're beautiful because I love you."

Geoff kissed him softly, and they watched the snow fall in the fading light.

Andrew Grey

The prequel to *Love Means... No Shame*

By Andrew Grey

Love Means... COURAGE

Len Parker is laid off during the recession in the early eighties and decides to go back to college at home in rural Michigan, where he reconnects with his best friend from high school, Ruby. He's overjoyed when she marries Cliff Laughton and overcome with sorrow when she dies an untimely death, leaving behind her husband and two-year-old son.

Out of work again, Len finds a job at Cliff Laughton's sorely neglected farm. Cliff is still mourning his wife, struggling to raise his son, and has little enthusiasm or energy left for work. Len immediately begins to whip the farm—including the two Laughtons—into shape. Working side by side, Len and Cliff grow ever closer, but loving another man takes a lot of courage. They'll have to stand together as they face faltering business, threatening drought, misguided family, and Midwestern prejudices to protect what might be a lifelong love.

Also Available from Dreamspinner Press

Don't miss the Children of Bacchus Series
by ANDREW GREY

ANDREW GREY grew up in western Michigan with a father who loved to tell stories and a mother who loved to read them. Since then he has lived throughout the country and traveled throughout the world. He has a master's degree from the University of Wisconsin-Milwaukee and works in information systems for a large corporation. Andrew's hobbies include collecting antiques, gardening, and leaving his dirty dishes anywhere but in the sink (particularly when writing). He considers himself blessed with an accepting family, fantastic friends, and the world's most supportive and loving partner. Andrew currently lives in beautiful historic Carlisle, Pennsylvania.

Visit his Web Site at http://www.andrewgreybooks.com and his blog at http://andrewgreybooks.livejournal.com/.

CPSIA information can be obtained at www.ICGtesting.com
Printed in the USA
LVOW102353050313

322844LV00031B/2139/P